OTHER BOOKS BY AUROR

Pentalogy of Hell
Book One: Iscariot
Book Two: Forty Days
Book Three: Lake of Fire
Book Four: The False Prophet
Book Five: The Son of Perdition

Abnormal Murders
Book One: Serial Killers with Cookies
Book Two: The Morph Suit Murderer
Book Three: The Flip Flop Felony

Tinon
Book One: Circus Wings
Book Two: Royal Blood
Book Three: Bandit Born

Aughts Boys
Book One: One More Sad Song
Book Two: The Horror at Camp New Woods
Book Three: Right or Wrong
Book Four: Hit or Miss
Book Five: Until I Fall Away

Vendettic
Book One: Spahn
Book Two: Sacrifice
Book Three: Sunset

New Match
Book One: New Match

Columbiner
The Crucifixion of Craig Knox
Beyr
Carl & Jimmy
Like Hell
Life in Anachronism
Rewind
Graduation Day
Truth or Dare

Guillaume

Aurora Dimitre

Copyright 2024

Cover by Larisa Katz

For everyone the Tumblr Lord of the Flies fandom circa 2014.

Guillaume

Part One: Ashton Collins

Let's Get the Story Straight

. chapter one .

Whenever I am called on to share a fun fact about myself, whether it be for meeting new people or first-day-of-school activities, I always use the island. What I don't mention is that I was close with Guillaume.

The short story is this: six years ago, when we were all twelve or thirteen years old, our plane crashed on a deserted island. Forty-two of us survived the crash. Fifteen of us came home. The reason the rest of them didn't isn't because of poisonous snakes, or spiders, or good old starvation. The reason was Guillaume.

My friendship with Guillaume is something I don't mention when bringing up the island because Guillaume is the reason the Bolin Disaster became the Bolin Tragedy, and I was the one propping him up the whole way.

That isn't something you tell people.

Lucky for me, I got away with it. Everyone was either so exhausted or tragic or confused that they forgot that where Guillaume had been, I was there, too. I even testified against him at the trial. Lucky for Guillaume, his father had enough money to hire a lawyer good enough to get him placed under psychiatric care until he turned eighteen. So six years after the island, he would be free. I have spent my six years as happily as I could have. I'm thinner than I was. I feel like it was one way or another with us island survivors: upon returning to the States, we either gorged ourselves on the sheer mass of food that was available to use, or we couldn't stomach it. I was the latter.

But other than that, I was fine. I finished middle school and I finished high school and I got accepted into every college I applied to. I think all of us did. There were only a select few boys who could capitalize on our tragedy, and capitalize we did. Most of us got talk shows, even. None of them were very big ones, except the ones that Kevin and Adam went on—but talk shows are talk shows. I'm sure some of us will come out with books as we get older, too.

  The college I decided on was one I'd wanted to go to since I'd been young. It was my mother's alma mater, a private liberal arts college in New England, and I was going to study political science. A few months before the school year started, I opened an e-mail from the school that was supposed to tell me who my roommate was going to be, and I do not lie when I say that my heart nearly stopped when I saw the name:

GUILLAUME ARGOT

×

It was stupid of me to assume that, just because he was crazy, his dad couldn't buy him into college. Whatever amount of money you're thinking the Argots have, they have more. Guillaume's imprisonment after the island had been very much a gilded cage; I did, at one point, look it up out of pure curiosity, and even though the image of an asylum is a pervasive one, with straightjackets, padded rooms, and electroshock therapy, that was not the case with Guillaume's experience. Guillaume had a private room, wore his own clothes, and spent most of his time in the library. He did high school over the internet and received a diploma in the mail.

  Part of me wanted to believe that my future roommate was some other Guillaume, but how many

Guillaume Argots are there in the world? Guillaume Argots going to an American college? A small, private liberal arts school that Guillaume, *my* Guillaume would have known... but other Guillaumes may not have?

I heard my parents coming up the stairs. I shut my laptop.

"Did you get the e-mail? Who's your roommate?" my mother asked.

"Roger," I said, because it seemed like a fairly harmless name. "Roger Elwin. I'm going to see if I can find him on Facebook or something tonight."

Roger Elwin was a name my mother could buy. Roger Elwin was probably blond, tall, broad-shouldered, played basketball or football, was going into something employable. The antithesis of Guillaume. Guillaume, if he was like he had been six years ago, was small, and skinny, and black-haired, and was likely going to get a degree in literature. When you were as rich as the Argot family, you could afford to get a passion degree. I was going to go for political science, but then go on to law school. My mother was a lawyer, and my father was a lawyer, and I would be a lawyer. Guillaume would learn about literature and then probably go on getting advanced degrees until he went to jail for real.

You could ask me why I didn't tell my mother about Guillaume. Why I didn't defer for a year, or go to a different college; a better college, even. Why I didn't call the admissions office or whoever was in charge of pairing up roommates and tell them that I couldn't room with Guillaume because when we were twelve we killed kids together. I would say that I froze, or that I didn't want to defer enrollment, or that I believed it wasn't my Guillaume, and all of that would be a lie. The reason I didn't do any of that was a mix of curiosity and guilt.

Curiosity, because I wanted to see what had become of him. I wanted to see if he was still the same, in looks and temperament, and in the little things that made Guillaume, Guillaume. The insane sweet tooth that, if his parents hadn't been richer than God, would have bankrupted his parents on dental bills. The fact that he would read anything and everything you put in front of him: nonfiction, fiction, it didn't matter. The one physical flaw I remembered—no matter how much sleep he got, he always had dark crescents under his eyes, like he needed about four more hours of rest.

And guilt, because I'd testified against him and gotten away scot-free.

. chapter two .

Hopefully, I thought, *Guillaume will be smart enough to stay away from the room until my parents leave.*

    I didn't know if he still looked the same, but I figured he'd look similar *enough* that if my parents saw him, they would recognize him; apart from the fact that his picture had been in the news for months, back when we were rescued, he'd spent a good handful of afternoons at my house. We spent more time at his, of course; it was larger and, usually, had less supervision, but we spent enough time at mine that my parents should recognize him. I thought it some kind of serendipity—or some kind of cash passing hands—that had kept his picture out of the papers upon his release.

    The dorm room we were moving into was the usual kind: communal bathrooms, extra-long twin beds, barely enough room for one person, let alone two. Desks and small closets and dressers. My father was carrying up my minifridge. "Did you talk to your roommate?" Mom asked. "Tell him that you had a fridge and a microwave?"

    "I couldn't find him online," I said, which was true. Guillaume did not have any social media, at least not under his own name. I guess it's possible that he had some Twitter or Instagram where he didn't post his face or use his real name, but he had nothing I could find.

    "Well," Mom said. She looked around. Guillaume had clearly already moved in. There were clothes hanging in one closet—all black. There were sheets on the bed—black—and a blanket—red. There were a dozen books stacked on top of the desk. I went over and looked at them. They were in alphabetical order by the author's last name.

×

They were:
    Girl on the Shore by Inio Asano
    The Inhuman Condition by Clive Barker
    The Exorcist by William Peter Blatty
    Lord of the Flies by William Golding
    The Only Good Indians by Stephen Graham Jones
    The Long Walk by Stephen King
    The Lost by Jack Ketchum
    The Cellar by Richard Laymon
    Frankenstein by Mary Shelley
    The House Next Door by Anne Rivers Siddons
    Perfume by Patrick Suskind
    Exquisite Corpse by Poppy Z Brite

×

I didn't know the books, but I figured they were scary. Guillaume read everything, but he liked horror the best. I remembered him having that proclivity for Clive Barker, back when we were young. He'd found a book by the man in a secondhand shop and had torn through it in just a few hours, not even getting up when I tried to bribe him with Mike'n'Ikes.

"Do you need anything else?" Mom asked. "Are you sure you don't want us to take you out to eat one last time?"

"No, I'm fine," I said. Dad clapped me on the shoulder and Mom hugged me.

"At least let me make your bed for you," she said.

I nodded, and she made my bed, and then she hugged me again, and then they were gone. I rambled in a soft circle before sitting down on my bed and staring at Guillaume's desk. I figured he'd be back any second now.

The door opened.

I looked.

There he was, just the same as ever: short, slim, dark hair that fell down over his eyes, which were large, and dark, and bottomless, and empty. Dark skin under his eyes. He had a slushie. It was blue: bright blue, and I wondered what godawful flavor it was. Cotton candy? Some Mountain Dew shit?

My heart had picked up its pace.

"Ashton," he said, finally.

"Gill," I replied, and that, actually, caused a flicker of something in his face. I was the only one who called him Gill: the first time I'd met him had been when I'd transferred to his school in the fifth grade. Our desks had been next to each other and I'd tried to read his desk tag and that had, for a ten-year-old who didn't have a great grasp on French phonics, led to me mispronouncing Guillaume.

To be fair, nobody could pronounce Guillaume right on the first try, because none of us really knew anything about French phonics, but I was the only one he let call him Gill. Everyone else got thumbtacks in their shoes if they did.

"I'm surprised you came," Guillaume said. "I figured you'd accepted here because this college was the only one that said my roommate assignment was OK, but I thought once you saw my name you'd back out."

"How'd you manage it?" I asked.

"I'd like to say it was chance," Guillaume said. He stepped into the room and let the door swing shut behind him. The way he talked was languid. He took breaks to drink his slushie. He kept moving toward me and I wanted to run but something kept me pinned to the bed. "That would be serendipity at its finest. But no. I knew you'd come to some private liberal arts school on the east coast. I applied to all of them. Put your name down as a roommate.

You wouldn't believe the amount of application fees I shelled out."

"Guillaume's daddy is rich," I said, trying out a crack from middle school. Guillaume didn't get mad, or laugh, or anything. He just tipped his head toward me in acknowledgement. "So you... what? Just on the off chance?"

"Yeah," Guillaume said. "I figured it was a long shot. You could've changed."

"I didn't," I said, and Guillaume nodded, a few times. He clearly hadn't, either. The slushie, even, was proof of that.

"What are you going for?" Guillaume asked. He crossed to his desk and dropped a slushie beside his stack of books, and then he turned and leaned on the desk, his feet coming off the ground briefly.

"Political science," I said.

"To law school?" Guillaume guessed, and I nodded. "How long before you switch to English?"

"I'm not switching to English," I said.

"I'm doing English."

If I hadn't changed, it was easy to see why he thought I would switch to English. In middle school I had done everything that Guillaume did. Same food, wore our ties the same way, took the same electives, were in the same groups—except football. I'd played football and he hadn't. Other than that, though, I followed him everywhere. It was a strange pairing, the class clown and the class freak, but I was enamored with him. Had been.

Of course that boy, the one who followed him everywhere, would switch to English.

"I'm not switching to English," I said again, and Guillaume shrugged one shoulder. He seemed tense, somehow. Like he'd wanted this, sure, but wasn't sure what to do with it now that he had it.

"Law school would take English, too," he said, finally, and then turned to face his desk, effectively dismissing me.

. chapter three .

The first month of college was as normal as it could be. Guillaume and I saw very little of each other. We both had morning classes and study groups in the afternoons—study groups or kept time studying in the library, alone, surrounded by dusty books, which was what I imagined for Guillaume. We didn't have a single class together. Not even generals. I was sure he'd taken dual-credit, online courses, so he probably had been able to skip the freshman composition class I was currently slogging my way through. He was always gone until long after I was asleep, and he was always asleep when I left to go to the gym in the morning. That was how Guillaume had always been: night owl.

    I grew complacent.
    I started to think of him as any other roommate. One I didn't see often, and one I didn't know anymore. He left candy wrappers everywhere and I had to take out his trash a few times because he had half-full pints of molding ice cream in it. It was irritating but nothing I was going to confront him over. If he'd lasted a few more months ignoring me, maybe I would have.
    But then he interrupted my lunchtime.
    I'd made friends in college. None were close friends, but they were friends I could eat with or partner with for projects or go to the twenty-four-hour diner at two in the morning with. I was eating with a few of them: Scott King, Emma Asimov, and Robert Tallis.
    "Ashton," Guillaume said, appearing at the end of the table. "Come eat with me."
    "You could sit with us?" Emma tried.
    I was already halfway to standing. "I'll catch up with you guys later," I said, and they all gave me awkward

smiles and waves and I knew that it wasn't going to be the same. By now, the fact that Guillaume was here had spread. The fact that he was living with me was also common knowledge, and anyone who looked up a list of survivors of the Bolin Tragedy would put two and two together and know that I had survived the island, too.

Granted, Ashton Collins is not like Guillaume Argot—there are definitely more Ashton Collinses in the United States. But the age, the location, the willingness to room with Guillaume…

I followed Guillaume to a corner table. Guillaume sat with his back to the room. I sat beside him instead of across from him. It was a habit from our schooldays.

As soon as I sat down, he started talking, fast and low, like he was afraid I'd get up and run.

"I have Ryan Spencer's address," he said, a little breathless, pulling a piece of paper out of his pocket. "He's not going to college, which checks out, he was always fucking dumb, but—"

"Gill," I said. "Why?"

Guillaume looked at me, then, like I was the stupidest motherfucker in the universe. "So we can finish what we started. Get them—"

"*Them*—"

"—look," Guillaume said, unfolding the paper and turning it into two. The one I only caught a glimpse of; from what I saw, it was a list. The other one was an address. "His family moved across town into a bigger house, and he's got siblings now, but it's within driving distance. We could do it this weekend."

"I'm not going to start killing people with you," I said, and he looked at me. Looked at me dead in the eyes, gave me that dead-fish stare that he'd scared the reporters with during his trial, and then he grabbed his butter knife. I leaned away from him, even though I wasn't really sure what kind of damage he could do with a butter knife—I knew enough not to underestimate Guillaume. It's not physical strength, a lot of the time, that says what someone can do to another person. It's willingness.

And Guillaume had always had plenty of that.

But instead of stabbing me, he brought the knife down to the back of his hand and ripped it through his skin. It wasn't a neat cut; it was jagged, because the butter knife was not meant to cut like that. But Guillaume gritted his teeth and dragged it through his skin, which seemed paper-thin, wispy, and as soon as I saw the blood welling up, I grabbed a napkin, batted the knife away, and pressed down as hard as I could. Red welled up through the napkin. I could see it, I could feel it, and I could smell it. It was making me feel lightheaded; the only thing anchoring me to this earth was the warmth coming up from Guillaume's hands, the wetness of his blood under my fingers.

"Stop."

"If you won't let me hurt someone else," Guillaume said, almost patiently, like I was some kind of little kid or something. "I'll hurt myself. They figured that out when I was locked up. I need to hurt someone. It's usually best if it's me."

×

That night, Guillaume showed me his scars.

He stood in front of me in his underwear, arms closed, arms spread. There were nicks and cuts from his wrist to his shoulder; his knee to disappear under his underwear; his stomach; his chest. His back was bare, probably because he couldn't reach it.

"You did all this?"

"Yes," Guillaume said. His lips barely parted as he spoke. That one word came out in an exhalation: *yes*.

"Nobody hurt you? Just you?"

One of Guillaume's eyes flicked open. "You are just dying to give me an excuse, aren't you? Yes, just me. All of these are from me. I did them because I needed to. Most of them. I suppose some of them are ones I got naturally on the island. But that wasn't anyone's fault, either."

I kept looking. Guillaume's eye closed again. Guillaume was pale, and the scars were paler. Little cuts, none of them big enough to really have been a danger to him, apart from one nasty one on his knee, which I remembered from the island.

All the other ones did look self-inflicted. Self-inflicted by someone who knew what they were doing.

"Nobody has ever hurt me," Guillaume said. "Nobody's fucking dared, honestly. I don't know if anyone can."

"I could," I said, and Guillaume gave me a look. "I could. I outweigh you by about forty pounds, Gill. I could do whatever I wanted to do."

"Then do it," Guillaume said.

"What?"

Both of Guillaume's eyes were open now, boring into my soul, and his arms slowly floated back down to his side. "Do it," he said. "Hurt me until I beg you to stop. I want to know if you can. And if you can, I want to know how it feels. Do it."

"Gill—"

"Do it," Guillaume said. "You said you could. So prove it."

I hesitated, but before Guillaume could say anything else I punched him in the jaw. It didn't have my full strength behind it; I knew that if you hit someone right there, that could be a knock-out button, but Guillaume staggered, a little, spat blood, and grinned. It was that shark grin, the one he'd used to get on the island when someone was caught, and even though I was the one doing the hurting here, I felt like one of the rabbits we'd hunted on the island, helplessly kicking while one of us, either me or Guillaume, came forward with the knife.

So I hit him again. In the stomach this time, harder this time, and he dropped to his hands and knees. I could hear his breathing, raspy, as he tried to start going again, and I hesitated.

"Keep going," he said. He spat blood again. I could see a string of it dripping to the floor.

I kicked him onto his back and sat on his stomach, my knees pinning his elbows to the floor. He looked up at me, a little dazed; his chest was rising and falling a little shallower than usual, probably because he wasn't getting enough air. Blood was still running from the corner of his mouth. I stared down at him. I didn't do anything but sit and stare.

"Are you done?" he asked. "I haven't begged you to stop yet."

I glanced up then. We were by his desk, and all of his shower stuff was on it. I stretched to reach his straight-razor—why he had it, I didn't know, because I didn't think he grew much, if any, facial hair—and I felt him wince, a little, when I put extra weight on his elbows. His eyes tracked my movements, and he flinched again; not a lot, but a little, when I brought the razor in front of his eyes.

He tracked it. I pressed it to his temple.

"You don't want to have to take me to the emergency room. I can't drive. You'd have to take me."

Grinning, I stood up and tossed the razor back onto his desk. He propped himself up on one elbow and wiped blood away from his mouth. "I haven't—"

"That was you begging," I said. "Logicking your way out of it is begging. You're never going to beg me to stop, but you will make me want to stop on my own." I crossed to sit on my bed. Guillaume pushed himself to his feet. He kept looking at the blood on his fingers like he'd never seen his own blood before—which, based on the scars that had *started* this whole thing, was ridiculous. "How did it feel?"

"What?"

"How did it feel getting hurt?"

He took his time answering that one. "I don't know," he said. "It was weird. I knew you wouldn't... I knew you wouldn't really hurt me."

"Then why did you ask me to stop?"

Guillaume was quiet at that one. "I don't know," he said, finally.

"Don't get me wrong," I said. "It was no, no Efrain Foley begging you to not disembowel him in front of a fire, but for you it was intense. The most I've ever seen from you, really."

"I know," he said. He shuddered, a little, and wiped blood from his mouth again.

"Does it change your mind, at all?"

"About what?"

"About doing this," I said. "Now that you've been hurt."

Guillaume was long in answering that one, and really, I think I knew his answer even before he said it. He shook his head, languid again, and when he looked at me, he seemed to have some modicum of trust and respect for me, something he hadn't had since the island. After I testified against him...

I was back in his good graces.

"I don't," Guillaume said. "I want to go as soon as we can."

. chapter four .

So we went that weekend.
    Ryan really didn't live all that far away. It was eight hours by car, and I did have a nice car. The sheer amount of money I had at that point really cannot be overstated: between the settlement from the airline and the money I got for the talk show, and the fact that I'd been given damn near a full ride for college, I had the money to spend on a nice, new-ish SUV. It was a comfortable existence.
    I put Guillaume in charge of scrolling through my Spotify. He really wasn't a music guy; I don't know if it was the total lack of empathy or what, but he didn't listen to music. I know the courts painted him as this heavy-metal-freak, but that wasn't true at all. The music that he knew was heavy metal, but that was because heavy metal was my music.
    He settled in on *Ice Nine Kills*. "Jesus, Gill," I said. "A little morbid today, huh? We gotta go full horror-slasher?"
    "I don't even know this band," Guillaume muttered. "The therapists thought that heavy metal was a bad influence."
    "These guys are hardly heavy metal," I said. "More like, I dunno. Emocore or something."
    "None of the words you're saying are real words," Guillaume said, and I laughed. It was these moments, with Guillaume picking out music while we headed to a gas station to fill up on sugar, that were, I think, the worst, because they reminded me that, despite it all, I *liked* Guillaume. And, maybe more damning, he liked me too.
    "They are so real words," I said. "And, dude, you gotta listen to this album straight through. No shuffling.

I'm not even going to let us skip to 'Hip to be Scared.' It's about *American Psycho*."

"That's a good book," Guillaume said, and we kept driving.

×

We had to pull into a gas station around noon to fill up, and anyway, it was good news for our stomachs, and probably my own personal flesh, because Guillaume had started threatening to cannibalize me if we didn't stop for some regularly scheduled sweetness. This would have been an emptier threat from someone who had not previously cannibalized someone.

"I'll go get food," Guillaume said. "And pay for your gas."

"Good," I said, and started pumping gas. There was no way I was paying for my own gas on this murder spree. Especially not in the previously described high-end SUV, which ate gas like a motherfucker.

I finished pumping gas and then headed for the store, because even though Guillaume was paying and said he would grab food, I wanted to make sure there were some Cheetos involved. A man could not subsist on sugary snacks alone.

But when I got in there, Guillaume was nowhere to be seen.

I went up to the guy behind the counter.

"Hey, did another kid come in here? Short, skinny, dark hair?"

The man was flipping through some magazine and he hardly even looked up. "Nope," he said.

"Seriously, he didn't disappear," I said. "He came in here to pay for gas and—"

"Gas's paid for."

"What?"

"Gas's paid for," the guy, his name tag read Scott, said. "Go on your way."

Yeah, so that just screamed something was fucky. I frowned at him, checked both bathrooms, really quick; luckily, the gas station was deserted, so I didn't get to add 'actual pervert' to my list of crimes. Then I headed outside to circle the gas station, figuring that he had to be out back, probably with something bad going on.

There was something bad going on. Guillaume was on the ground with blood around his mouth, but I was pretty sure it wasn't his blood, mostly because there were three other guys there, and one of them was also on the ground and screaming about his ear.

"What the fuck?" I said.

The two that had Guillaume pinned and were currently whaling on him like it was their job glanced back. "Your gas is paid for," one of them said.

"I heard," I said. "And I repeat: what the fuck?"

Guillaume wriggled and one of them kicked him in the ribs. He closed his eyes briefly, which was probably Guillaume-speak for '*holy-shit-ow-that-hurt-so-fucking-much.*' I took a step forward.

Suddenly, the one who had been crying about his ear spoke up. "Hey, aren't you one of those kids, too? I remember watching your testimony."

. chapter five .

"I should've bleached my hair or something," Guillaume said as we piled back into the car, both of us a little worse for wear. "I still look like I did when I was twelve. Those guys recognized me *immediately*."

"Well," I said, trying to keep up my good spirits even though those guys might've cracked a rib or two. "At least we got free gas out of the deal."

"Yeah, but we have to get snacks still," Guillaume said, and he stared sullenly out the window as I took us to the next gas station down the road. This time I went in with him and he put his hood up. I didn't ask him how it had gone down. If they'd cornered him or if they'd said something to lure him outside—all I knew was that he'd bitten an ear off of a guy, which would have been shocking if it wasn't a repeat trick.

Those guys must have recognized him immediately.

Really, it shouldn't have surprised me. I must have just been lulled into some false sense of security by the fact that, even though everyone on campus *knew*, there had been no incidents, apart from a couple of psych majors trying to be his friend and failing miserably. But Guillaume was still recognizable. No matter how much money his dad had paid to keep his current, adult face out of the media, his twelve-year-old face had been everywhere.

And Guillaume did, like he'd said, look pretty much the same as he had when he was twelve.

Guillaume gathered all of the shit he needed: cherry sours, gummy bears, Nerds ropes, and a couple of chocolate candies thrown in there for variety. Guillaume had always been more about the fruity candy than anything else. He also went for a slushie. I grabbed some chips and jerky, as well as a Mountain Dew energy drink from the back fridge and a piece of pizza from the 'real food' area. We took it all up to the front counter and Guillaume paid cash. The guy behind the counter didn't take any notice of us.

"You're going to get sick," I said as we made our way back to the car. Guillaume had the bag of snacks swinging from his hand and he was humming, a little. It was the happiest I'd seen him in a while. I didn't want to think about the fact that he'd bitten a guy's ear off was probably the reason for his good mood. I wanted to pretend that it was just because of the slushie.

"I've got a system figured out by now," Guillaume said. "The first couple days out I did get sick. But I know how to control myself now."

"I don't understand how you're not four hundred pounds," I muttered as I pulled myself up into the driver's side seat. "Your calorie needs cannot be that much."

Guillaume shrugged and I cracked the energy drink.

"So," I said. "What's the plan?"

x

The plan, as Guillaume outlined it:
1. Drive most of the way on Saturday. Stay overnight in a motel.
2. Finish up the drive on Sunday. With no further incidents, we should be there before noon.
3. Guillaume had done some online stalking and had found out that, normally, on Sundays, the Spencers would go to the park. Normally, this was just the younger siblings and the parents, leaving Ryan alone in the house.
4. Here we didn't want to get too down and dirty with the details, because, as Guillaume said, "The fun is really in the improvisation."

x

Watching Guillaume navigate the internet was always fun, simply because it was very clear that, while he could handle the limited amount of websites that the institution had allowed him to access to do his homework, social media absolutely baffled him. He'd made a Facebook and an Instagram to better stalk Ryan's friends and family, and he kept getting annoyed by the ads.

"I hate this," he muttered. "I hate this so much. This is so useless. I can't find out the *information I'm trying to see because they keep trying to sell me coffee.*"

"Welcome to the internet, Gill," I said. "I don't even mess with social media."

"Yeah, but everyone's mom does," Guillaume said. We were in the hotel room at that point. Guillaume was on his phone, which was, naturally, the newest iPhone, paid for by Daddy's money. He was clumsy with a touchscreen, too—the computer he'd used to graduate high school had been a desktop. In terms of technology, Guillaume had tapped out about six years ago.

We'd gotten a two-bed room (also paid for with Daddy's money), and I wanted to ask Guillaume if Daddy would, say, ask why Guillaume was spending money on a hotel room, but I figured that Daddy probably just didn't want to ask questions about his only son who was a psychopath. I was flipping through channels on one bed and Guillaume was fighting Mark Zuckerberg on the other.

"Fuck," Guillaume muttered. "I accidentally clicked it."

Then there was a weight beside me and Guillaume handed the phone over. "What?" I said.

"Get me out of this ad hell," he said. "Is there a way I can pay and not have to see them?"

"Not on Instagram, I don't think," I said. I did get him out of where he was clearly about halfway through ordering… lingerie? Who the hell did Guillaume's

Instagram think he was? I guess he was only following the mothers of our not-yet-deceased classmates, so maybe they thought he was also a woman in her forties, which would, I guess, explain the coffee and lingerie ads. "You know, if you made an actual account, with your face, where you posted pictures and stuff, I bet you'd do some numbers. There are a ton of girls who want to fix you."

"There are a ton of stupid girls, then," Guillaume said. "How do you know this?"

"Because there are girls who tried to fix me, and they didn't even know I was your best friend," I said. "Tragedy *does* something to some girls. I lost my virginity when I was like fourteen."

"Seriously?" Guillaume said. "I thought you were unique."

"What do you mean?"

"About liking me," Guillaume said. "I thought you were unique about liking me. Turns out you're just like those stupid girls."

It was quiet for a second, and then I said, "I'm putting you back in ad hell."

. chapter six .

We left early the next morning. Breakfast was, for me, what I could grab from the continental breakfast as they were setting up, and for Guillaume, a Reese's from the vending machine, washed down with a strawberry Fanta from a different vending machine. We put on some music as we went. Guillaume fiddled around with my Spotify and came up with "Killer Klowns" by *The Dickies*. "Remember when we watched this movie?" he asked.
    "It was so dumb," he muttered.
    "You loved it," he said. "I thought it was dumb."
    "You're the one who made us watch it like six times," I said, and his mouth was tinged red from the Fanta and I was reminded of him a day ago, spitting blood that wasn't his out of his mouth. I had never asked what had happened to the ear, because it sure wasn't on the guy's head anymore, and that meant, to me, that I was pretty sure that Guillaume had *eaten* it, *swallowed it whole*, and again, this wasn't a *new thing*, but—
    But here we were, joking about *Killer Klowns from Outer Space*, and he'd eaten a guy's ear less than twenty-four hours ago. It scared me how quickly I was falling back into a rapport with him. How much I *liked* him. It made me think that maybe the island hadn't just been a fluke. That there really was something majorly fucking wrong with me.
    But of course there was. I was going along with this shit, remember.

×

We pulled up about two blocks from Ryan's house and I parked the car. We figured that the possibility of a quick escape was less important than someone make the connection between my license plates + murder, so the idea was that we could kill Ryan without too much notice and then drive off all nice and normal. We even had changes of clothes in my backpack; T-shirts, for sure, but even pants and shoes. Like, we were about to do this right.

Guillaume also had a knife. Just one. It looked awful similar to the one he'd had on the island. I was sure it wasn't the same one—that one had to be in police evidence somewhere, locked up, somewhere Guillaume could never get it again—but this one looked the same size. Serrated blade, just like the other one. Serrated blade because it was crueler. It ripped through skin instead of sliding through it.

"A-fucking-ha," Guillaume muttered. He passed the phone over. It was an Instagram picture of Ryan Spencer's mom, dad, and two little sisters. "Someone's alone at home and ready to die."

"Okay," I said. I passed the phone back. He stuck it in his hoodie pocket and we headed out.

×

Ryan Spencer was a dumbass.

That was something we had always known. He was somewhat of a bully; back in school, back when we were twelve, he'd spent his time tripping kids like Laurence Dale, who was the fattest kid in our class, and had asthma, even (though we were all pretty sure he'd made that up because he didn't want to participate in gym class), or shoving Sage Horton's head down the toilet, because Sage Horton's dad was in jail for hitting Sage and his mom and as such Sage was *real* jumpy and *real* easy to scare. Ryan had never gone after me because I was the funny one and he'd never gone after Guillaume because Guillaume was creepy and richer than God.

Laurence and Sage had both died on the island. Laurence had died first, out of all of us that survived the plane crash. Sage had died begging for us to kill him. If you looked up any of the documentaries about the island, you would see their faces: Laurence's chubby but smiling; a blond, ruddy kid who liked to read and play computer games, and Sage, small and unsure of himself, olive-toned, looking more worried than anything else. Laurence had died a lot faster than Sage had. Sage had, maybe because of his dad, some kind of toughness to him that had made him tough to crack, physically, at least. Psychologically he was a mess. But physically he was able to take a lot of damage and keep ticking. You could tell he wished he wasn't that tough, though, able to beg for death all streaked with blood, missing most of one arm. Sage had died during Guillaume's disembowelment stage, but at the end of it; you could tell that Guillaume had been trying to beat someone to death, but he really shouldn't have gone with someone who was that used to being hit. Watching Sage get hit was like watching a basketball player when someone tossed him the ball: he plain knew what to do.

That made me sound callous, but to be frank, if I couldn't think about it plainly like that, I would go nuts.

But Ryan was a dick. His records were what Guillaume's lawyers had pulled up, mentioning all the times Ryan had gotten sent to the principal's, all the times Ryan had gotten suspended, for being violent with his classmates. He was really the one that, after Guillaume, everyone was probably the most scared of, because he was bigger than the rest of us and definitely enjoyed it. And in the early days of the island, before Guillaume really got going, he was the bad guy. Kevin's enforcer. Before Guillaume really got going, that was the big question: Kevin versus Adam, who was the better leader? It was Adam, but then he got to be too much of a nag and *that* was when Kevin took over. It also helped that Kevin was the leader of a group of football guys—myself included—and they would do whatever he said. Not that I did whatever Kevin said. I actually kind of liked Adam.

I did whatever Guillaume said, though, which was probably worse.

×

The Spencer house was huge. Most of the kids who crash-landed on the island were rich; the few who weren't were there on scholarship. It was a private school. We crashed in ties.

You could tell that Guillaume didn't really think much of it, though. Like I said, Guillaume = richer than God. This was probably the same size as the Argots' quaint little summer cabin, or whatever. It was pretty big, though. As the son of two lawyers who weren't necessarily big-shot lawyers, I thought it was big enough.

Ryan wasn't downstairs or anything so easy, but we could hear rap music coming from upstairs. The back door was unlocked. We literally just walked into the backyard, through a backyard fence that latched on the outside, past a dog that wagged its tail lazily at us, and walked in through the back door. We came out in a kitchen.

I shut the door softly.

"You ready?" Guillaume asked, his voice pitched low. He was practically trembling.

God, he looked excited.

I nodded. There was something unfolding in my stomach; anticipation, I thought. I didn't know if it was excitement or fear, though. Maybe a little of both. This did, for lack of a better term, take me back.

We walked as quietly as we could through the house. It was a newer house, so it didn't creak much; still, it took us damn near five minutes to climb the stairs. I could tell that Guillaume wanted to just say fuck it and bound up the stairs, knife in hand, but he didn't. He crept. And I crept behind him.

It turned out that it didn't even matter. We got to Ryan's bedroom door, which was wide open, and he was playing video games with his back to the door, rap music blasting through his soundbar. He didn't even glance back.

Guillaume grinned at me. It was the shark grin. Then he walked over and put the knife under Ryan's throat. "Hey, Spence," he said, almost conversationally. "Long time no see."

. chapter seven .

Ryan tried to jerk away, but Guillaume caught him by the hair and yanked his head back so that Ryan could look him in the eyes. "*Argot?*" Ryan said.

"The one and only," Guillaume said. "Well, not the one. C'mon, Ash, get in here."

Ryan tried to twist to see me, too, but Guillaume didn't let him. The knife was still poking into his neckflesh and Guillaume still had a hand in his hair. I crossed to the bed, a bit closer to where Ryan was sitting, on a beanbag.

"*Collins?*" Ryan said.

I didn't say anything.

"All right, Ryan," Guillaume said. "It is very important that you answer this for us. How long does your mom's Sunday picnic normally last?"

"Wh—how do you—"

"Your mom loves Instagram," Guillaume said. "I do, too. It helped me figure out when you would be alone. Don't scream or it'll hurt worse."

Ryan swallowed, hard; I could see his Adam's apple bob. Guillaume was tracing the knife now, almost tickling it up and down Ryan's neck. I crossed to the TV and turned up the music. Guillaume gave me an appreciative look.

"Too bad he doesn't listen to your heavy metal crap, Ash," Guillaume said. "There's tons of screaming in those songs. Hey, go find a sock or something."

Ryan broke away, then, jerking his head out of Guillaume's grip, leaving behind a hunk of hair, and caught me at the knees. I went down. Like I said, after the island, we either bulked up with the sheer amount of food and food choices in the real world, or we couldn't eat because of the horrors or whatever, and I was the latter. Ryan was the former. He'd always been big, but now he was entering Laurence territory. Either way, I hit the ground hard, and Ryan scrabbled to grab me in a way that would maybe make Guillaume think twice about hurting him. We wrestled on the floor, and it reminded me of the locker room after football games when we'd win and were so hyped up that the floor was a mass of writhing with someone, eventually, coming out on top. Usually it was Ryan or Kevin.

But Ryan had me now, and this one ended with me, my face pressed into the floor, my arm jacked up so high that it felt like it was about to break. I gritted my teeth. "I'll break his arm if you come near me," Ryan said. His voice was scared. He was scared of Guillaume; so desperately, he was *scared of Guillaume*. His weight was on my back and I couldn't really breathe, between that and the fact that my nose was squished into the carpet, which, at the very least, seemed to have been vacuumed recently.

"Do it," Guillaume said. "You won't kill him. You wouldn't fucking dare."

"Don't *test* me," Ryan shrieked, and Guillaume must have approached because my arm wrenched higher. I squeezed my eyes shut. It was going to break. Guillaume was going to let it break, because we both knew, we *all* knew that Ryan wasn't going to kill me, and while Guillaume liked me, my pain was as delicious to him as anyone else's. At the very least, everything was starting to go a little fuzzy around the edges. I figured it was either because I wasn't getting anywhere near enough oxygen or because of the pain.

"I'll test you," Guillaume said. "Hey, Spence, do you dream about the island? Do you dream about killing Sage Horton? You were the one who did that final blow, right?"

"Because he—you wouldn't *kill him*, he was bleeding out, his guts were everywhere, and he was—he begged—"

"I don't think that holds up in a court of law," Guillaume said. "I mean, unless you have a scapegoat."

My arm went higher. It was screaming now. I passed out, briefly, but when I came to again it was more of the same so it might as well have not happened at all.

"Let him go," Guillaume said. "Are you scared of me? Ash can take me. If you can take Ash, you can take me. Logic."

My arm went.

Ryan scrambled away from me, like he wasn't really expecting to actually break my arm. The pain radiated from the break up and down my arm, down to my fingertips, up to my heart, to my collarbone. I pushed myself up on my good arm and leaned against the bed. "Jackass," I breathed.

"Damn it, Spence," Guillaume said. "You broke something of mine."

I used my good hand to shoot him the bird and he grinned at me. Even though I was hurt he was still in his element. Like I figured he would be. He advanced on Ryan, who stumbled backward, back into his TV, which hit the floor with a *crash*—I could see a spiderwebbing of cracks coming from the corner that had hit first. Everything was sharper, somehow, with the pain. The sweat running down my nose. The feeling of my T-shirt against my neck.

Ryan's breathing; harsh, staccato. Guillaume practically floating toward him like an angel.

Ryan must have figured, then, that his best bet was in attacking. And if he'd caught Guillaume by surprise he would have been able to take him. But Guillaume was ready, and when Ryan charged, he ducked and shoved him. Straight into me, which sucked; Ryan hit me like a bowling ball, his knee in my stomach, his other leg on my broken arm, his elbow in my face. I made a noise like a cat getting stepped on by a horse, but I figured I knew what Guillaume wanted. I grabbed onto Ryan's shirt with my good hand, holding it so tight I could feel my fingernails through the fabric. Ryan tried to scramble away, which also hurt; I was what he was scrambling on, and it was pure adrenaline and pure ~~love~~ obedience to Guillaume that kept me holding onto him.

Guillaume was behind him, then. His hand grabbed Ryan's hair, right at the hairline, and with his other hand, he ripped the knife across Ryan's throat. Ryan's blood spurted over me like a shower, hitting me in the face, the chest. Ryan's body convulsed. His shin pushed right on the break and I passed out.

. chapter eight .

I woke up to Guillaume wiping my face. "You're going to have to change shirts," he said.

We were still in Ryan's bedroom. Guillaume had pulled Ryan off of me and gone and changed himself. My arm throbbed. "Ow," I said.

"It's going to hurt worse," Guillaume said. "You're going to have to change shirts."

"Fuck you," I muttered. "Can't you cut me and say it's my blood?"

"Sure, until Ryan's type O and you're type A," Guillaume said. "And they test it, and suddenly we're... I'm in real jail this time. Especially with the wound you could probably get away scot-free again. I *did* use you."

"Does it scare you?" I asked. Guillaume was kneeling over me. The light was behind him. Again, it hit me that he looked like some kind of angel.

"What?"

"Real prison?" I said. Guillaume wiped more blood off of my face. It was all I could smell. Ryan Spencer's blood. We had killed Ryan Spencer. I had helped to kill Ryan Spencer and now my arm was broken and Guillaume Argot was wiping blood from my face.

"No," Guillaume said. "Nothing scares me."

×

Getting me into a new shirt had been painful. Guillaume had also taken the time to wipe down everything that might have fingerprints, unless we could take it with us, like the rag that he'd used to wipe my face. He stuck that in his back pocket where it fluttered, blood-stained white, like a failed surrender flag. I mostly tried not to pass out again. The break wasn't so bad that the bone was sticking out or anything, but it was bad enough to hurt. Eventually, though, Guillaume deemed it clean enough and we headed back to the car.

"You have to pretend you're not hurt," Guillaume said.

"I know," I said through gritted teeth. My arm jolted with every step I took, sending spikes of pain back down to my fingertips and up to my collarbone. My fingertips felt fuzzy. Asleep, almost. "I'm trying."

When we got to the car, Guillaume went over to the driver's side, leaving me to hoist myself into the passenger-side by myself. Fuck my parents for getting me this SUV that you had to climb into. I was breathing hard, sweating, had bit through the inside of my cheek and was bleeding from the corner of my mouth. Guillaume was pulling the seat up so he could reach the gas and the brake.

I managed enough coherence to say, "Gill, can you *drive*?"

"Theoretically," Guillaume said. He adjusted the mirrors. "You're going to have to wait on the hospital until we get back home."

"You just like seeing me in pain," I said. I was only half-joking.

"Sure," Guillaume said. "But it's mostly logical."

"Love you too, Argot," I muttered, and buckled myself, bit into my cheek again, spat blood in Guillaume's empty slushie cup, and let my eyes drift shut for the ride home. If Guillaume was breaking traffic laws and running over puppies, I didn't want to know.

. chapter nine .

After we killed Ryan Spencer, things went back to semi-normal. I had to make up a story for my classmates and my parents that I'd fallen down a set of stairs (I'd added *drunk* for my classmates and implied it for my parents) and that was how I'd broken my arm. I had enough secondary bruises to make it seem logical. Thank you, Ryan Spencer, for outweighing me by a hundred and twenty pounds. Guillaume read about ten books a week in the time after Ryan Spencer's death; we'd unofficially decided that while I had a cast, we would ignore the rest of the list. Guillaume also got his driver's license. He'd apparently done a half-decent job of getting us home the day we killed Ryan Spencer, but if he'd gotten pulled over we would've been in trouble.

But school went on. I enjoyed my classes. I reconnected with the few friends that I'd abandoned when Guillaume had come back to me—and I mean *really* come back to me—with his plan and with his list.

And then my parents found out that my roommate was Guillaume.

×

"Why didn't you tell us?" my mom said, over the phone, in lieu of a hello.

"Um," I said. "What?"

I had a neat forty-five minute break between classes, and I was outside, sitting on the grass behind the library. Mom had texted me and asked me if I was too busy for a call and I'd said no.

"About your roommate," my mom said. "Not only did you not tell us, but you *lied*."

"How did you…" I trailed off. *Shit*.

"Your dorm posted a picture on Instagram," my mom said. I bit down hard on my thumbnail and wished that I'd just shut the door in my RA's face when he'd come around to take a picture of the room. Guillaume wasn't even *in* the picture, but I'd seen the post, and it had both of our names in the caption. No last names, but last initials, and it had mentioned our majors, and probably from that…

"I didn't want you to freak out," I said. "Like you're doing right now."

"Freak out? Freak *out*? I don't even know what that university is doing, letting him *come*, let alone—"

"He's better now, Mom," I said. "He had some kind of psychotic break or something, on the island, but he's been institutionalized for six years and he's medicated and mostly he just sits around and reads."

Oh, and we went and killed Ryan Spencer a few weeks ago.

"I heard that the Spencer boy was killed a few weeks ago," Mom said.

"Gill *just* got his license," I said. "Like, a week ago. He doesn't even have a car yet. His dad is sending him one that's worth more than our house."

Except I drove him and I helped and that's how I broke my arm.

"How did you two get put together?" Mom asked.

I waited a beat. I didn't know what would be better, to lie about this, because who would believe serendipity, or to tell the truth, which made Guillaume sound like a psychopath. And he was. A psychopath, I mean.

But I was trying to convince my mother of the opposite.

"He requested me," I said. "He... I think he needed something. You know. Familiar. I was pretty much his only friend, before..."

"Before he killed thirty kids?"

"Mom, you know we all helped. If we really wanted to stop him, we could have. He was the smallest kid on the island," I said. She didn't respond to that, not right away, and I wondered if I'd made a mistake saying it. All of the parents, apart from the Argots, I guess, had been able to clutch to the one fact that, legally, *at least* their kids weren't the crazy ones, no matter how well they knew otherwise. Throwing this in my mother's face was probably not helping my case any. "Do you want to see our room? Do you want to see that he's just sitting around reading? I'll switch to a video call."

"That would make me feel better," she said, and I hung up on her. I sent a quick text to Guillaume to let him know that I'd be coming back with my mom on video, and he didn't respond. He had his read receipts on, though, so I knew he read it. It was mostly so that I didn't walk in on him naked or something—that's what I told myself. Maybe if I was lucky he'd take out his trash. He was back to his pint-of-ice-cream-a-night diet and the guy did not know how to clean up after himself.

I called my mom back. "I've got to walk back to the dorm," I said. "I'm outside."

"Okay," she said. I showed her the campus as I walked; the day I'd moved in, I'd been so focused on getting her and dad out of there before Guillaume showed up that I hadn't really showed her around or anything. It was her alma mater and everything, so it wasn't like she didn't know where everything was, but I was sure stuff had changed since her undergrad. It was small enough that I was back at my dorm in about five minutes, so I took her upstairs, up to the dorm, and when I cracked open the door, Guillaume was sprawled on his bed, reading a book by the Marquis de Sade.

I switched the view on the phone so that Mom could see the room and glared at him. He barely looked up at me. "So, this is the room," I said. "My closet, Gill's closet. My bed, Gill's bed. There's Gill—see, sitting there reading. Like I said. That's all he does. Um, my desk, Gill's desk, trash cans, under the beds—" I dropped to the floor so that she could see both under my bed and under Guillaume's bed, which mostly had boxes and packets of ramen noodles. "No corpses. No dead animals. Not even a contraband candle."

"Hello, Mrs. Collins," Guillaume said without looking up from his book. Guillaume usually wore a lot of black, and I was glad that he'd worn his one school T-shirt today. It looked like the free one they sent you when you were admitted. I wondered what the hell he was doing wearing a crappy free T-shirt when his dad had more money than God.

"Hi, Guillaume," my mom said. I switched the view back to look at me and sat down next to Guillaume on his bed, knocking the book down so he had to stop reading. Guillaume gave me a sideways look and I smiled at my mother. "How has your semester been going?"

"It's all right," Guillaume said. It was hard to tell over video, but my mother looked nervous. Like even seeing Guillaume over video made her want to run away screaming.

"I heard you were an English major?"

"Right," Guillaume said. He fidgeted, and I wondered how much longer he'd stand this. He *must* have gotten better at dealing with adults, or they never would have let him out… but, I remembered, before the island, most of our interactions with adults had been through me. I would talk to the adults, and Guillaume would stand behind me and look at the ground. He wasn't super social in general, but adults would ask him questions that his classmates *wouldn't*.

"That makes sense," my mother said. "Well, Ashton. I'll see you at Thanksgiving."

And then she was gone.

"She's pissed," I said, turning and situating myself nicely on Guillaume's bed, my feet on his lap, my head on his pillow. His forearms rested on my shins. He looked at me. I was being the kind of familiar that I had been before (and on) the island. We had gotten close again.

Killing a guy together did that to you, I guessed.

"Why didn't you tell her?" Guillaume said. "After you moved in, I mean."

"I thought I could keep it a secret," I said. "I didn't know that they'd take a picture of our room for social media."

"That was stupid," Guillaume said.

"Why are you reading the *Marquis de Sade*?" I asked. "That's the bigger question."

"He's good," Guillaume said. "*120 Days of Sodom* is worthless, the movie's way better, but *Justine* is good. It was actually finished."

I shook my head, staring up at the ceiling. Guillaume's warmth around my feet, the lower half of my legs, was distracting. I always thought of him as cold, practically dead already, but that wasn't true. He was warm. "Isn't the movie for that Sodom one on all those, most disturbing movies lists?" I asked.

"Are you telling me you haven't seen it?" Guillaume asked.

"It looked boring," I said.

Guillaume scoffed, deep in his throat, and then moved my feet to go and fetch his computer. I sat up, frowning. Was he about to make me watch this movie right now? I had class in twenty minutes. "Gill, I have class—"

"Skip it," Guillaume said. He had his computer under his arm and he stepped over me, tucking himself in-between me and the wall. "It's Friday, anyway. You don't have a test or anything, do you?"

"Well, no, but—"

"Then skip it," Guillaume said. He logged onto his computer. His background was our class picture from before the island and I swallowed and looked away until he had the movie pulled up. He tapped at his keyboard a little. "I don't suppose you speak Italian?"

"Guillaume, do *you* fucking speak Italian?"

"It's very close to French," Guillaume said. "I'm fluent in French. I watch this movie without subtitles all the time. Really, the dialogue isn't the important part."

×

The movie was weird. It was uncomfortable to watch, for sure; Guillaume *had* put on subtitles, perhaps because it was my first viewing, but it hardly seemed to matter. I'd thought his throwaway line about dialogue not being the important part was just because he liked to see people hurt and humiliated, and maybe it was right, but I had to admit he had a point. The dialogue didn't seem to matter.

The credits rolled. I glanced over at him. His color was high. He was biting down on the inside of his lip. I could see the tension in his face. "Did the movie turn you on, or something?"

He moved like a cat, knocking his laptop to the end of the bed and straddling me, his knees around my waist, his hands on my face, his lips on mine. I froze. His eyes were closed. He bit my lip deep enough to draw blood.

Then he was gone. Crashing down the hallway like he couldn't stand to be near me for any longer. I sat on his bed, abandoned, wild-eyed, before figuring I might as well go and get dinner. Not that I was super hungry after that movie—but a man had to eat.

When I got back, he still wasn't around. He had, however, come back. There was a note on my desk.

IT WASN'T THE MOVIE.
     ga
PS. (MAYBE A LITTLE BIT THE MOVIE)
PPS. (BUT THAT WASN'T THE MAIN REASON)

. chapter ten .

I wasn't really sure where our relationship stood after Guillaume kissed me and then, basically, admitted that I turned him on. He acted exactly the same. My cast came off right after Thanksgiving; it was a good excuse to only stay one night, and one night of fielding awkward questions about the fact that I was rooming with Guillaume Argot, *yes, that Guillaume Argot,* no he's not going to kill anyone, *yes, that Guillaume Argot,* was enough.

"I think that the next one should be someone easier to control," Guillaume said. "My thought was Ayers."

I considered it. Richard Ayers was someone that I had always been surprised survived the island. Richard Ayers was small, and too nice for his own good—naïve, probably, was a good word for him. He'd spent most of his time on the island digging around for bugs and lizards, living in an almost completely different reality than the rest of us. As a result, we'd pretty much left him alone. He hadn't lived with us, he hadn't eaten with us, and he hadn't been part of our games. The helicopter that spotted us and taken Adam away had sent a boat, and when that boat showed up, he'd picked his way out of the jungle and looked around owlishly at us, we who were covered in blood and all in shock, and had calmly boarded.

But if he'd stayed the same, he would be easy to control.

"All right," I said. "That seems reasonable. Do you know where he lives?"

"Yes," Guillaume said, grinning his shark grin. "He has a YouTube channel where he talks about plants and every time he does a Q&A he fields questions about the island. I watched every one of his videos. He's always going to a certain butterfly refuge."

Guillaume named it. I didn't recognize the name—then again, I didn't make it a habit to visit butterfly refuges. "So you don't know where he lives," I said.

"No," Guillaume said. "But I do know that he goes to this butterfly refuge."

"It's the middle of winter," I pointed out. "How far south are we going?"

×

The answer was Florida. "Christmas break is coming up," Guillaume said. "We're going to Florida for Christmas break. We don't even have to take your car. I'll get us plane tickets. We can go to Universal."

I looked at him, one eyebrow raised.

"Pictures, Ash," Guillaume said. "A reason to go. Remember, your poor roommate spent most of his teenage years in the psych ward. I didn't get to go to Harry Potter world with the rest of you."

Okay, there had been a few all-expense-paid trips to places like Disney World for those of us who had survived the island and were not named Guillaume Argot. Not all of us went. I went. I went, Ryan Spencer had gone, Erik Marsh… Richard Ayers had gone, too. I was sure there were one or two others that had gone, at least. Kevin and Adam had not; Kevin, because he was still seen as a secondary villain, as someone who had gotten away with it all because Guillaume had been there to take the fall, and Adam because it was too soon. He'd had a lot of physical therapy to go through.

"You think people are going to buy that?" I asked. "I mean, my mom had questions about Ryan Spencer."

"Sure, everyone will have questions," Guillaume said. "But I think me hanging out with you helps me. Nobody remembers what you did, Ash, except for you."

"And you," I said. "You remember."

"Well, yeah," Guillaume said. "I remember. But I'm crazy. I'm not a reliable witness."

"I'll have to talk to my parents," I said, finally. "I don't know what they'll say—"

"I'm paying, Ash," Guillaume said. "Besides, we really will go to Universal. We'll buy souvenirs. We'll ride the rides. We'll eat. We'll take a million pictures and you can put it on your new Instagram."

I'd made one recently. It was doing *numbers* with my candid shots of Gill.

"Save a few, right, for when we're killing Richard Ayers?" I said.

"We'll just nab him," Guillaume said, grinning. "Keep him in the truck or hotel or something while we go for our last day so we have an alibi."

I nodded, sighed, and went to go figure out how to convince my mother to let me go to Orlando with a psycho.

. chapter eleven .

My mother wasn't pleased, but she relented. "It's good for him," I'd said. "And besides, his parents are paying for everything. Hotel, snacks, souvenirs, plane tickets, everything."

Sometimes I feel like, when my mother looked at Guillaume (if I'd whined enough), she saw the kid that had lurked behind her son for a couple of years—I'd joined their school in the fifth grade, and we'd crashed at the end of our seventh grade year—before the plane went down and we were lost for a couple months. Guillaume had been bad then, too, but he'd also been a kid, and kids, in the eyes of most adults, were fixable. We'd used to look at the comments on his report cards, me and Guillaume, and look at them. The English teachers all loved him, because he read more than he was assigned for school, and all of the teachers admitted that, academically, he was as good or better than his classmates.

It was always the social skills that tripped them up.

GUILLAUME DOES NOT SEEM TO MAKE FRIENDS EASILY.

SOME STUDENTS REPORT FEELING AFRAID OF GUILLAUME.

GUILLAUME ONLY APPEARS TO HAVE ONE FRIEND. (That's me!)

GUILLAUME WOULD DO WELL TO REMEMBER
THAT HIS CLASSMATES ARE PEOPLE TOO AND
THAT HIS ACTIONS CAN HURT THEM.

Guillaume hadn't ever *really* hurt anyone before the island. He'd stolen stuff, and he'd set stuff on fire, and he'd killed animals—well, we'd killed animals—but the closest thing he'd done to hurting someone *bad* was shoving Sage Horton down the stairs—Sage because he was always so covered in bruises anyway—and nobody had even found out that had been him. It had been during a passing period and Guillaume had been in position and he'd shoved and Sage had gone down, bouncing, almost, to land in a heap at the bottom. He'd hardly made a sound. Protected his head and everything.

That had excited Guillaume, I remember. We'd talked about it when we were in his bedroom doing homework. "He knows how to fall," Guillaume had said. "How many stairs do you s'pose he's been tossed down? I wish I was stronger. I can only push."

But either way, we were going to head to the airport. We'd spend the entirety of Christmas break in Orlando. Richard Ayers didn't live in Orlando—but the butterfly sanctuary he liked was only an hour away. Guillaume had arranged a rental car for us, to shuttle us around, and we would wait for Richard to go live. When he did, we'd drop everything and head over there. We'd wait for him to be done.

Then we'd nab him. Keep him in the hotel room to have fun with when we weren't out being tourists.

I thought it was a solid plan and, despite my reservations about really going down Guillaume's dark road—like it wasn't already too late, LOL—I was excited. I tried to funnel that excitement into the idea that I was getting a free Florida vacation, but I kept trying to picture the look on Richard Ayers's face when he saw us. Probably he'd be smiley at first. Ayers had always been optimistic and friendly to everyone, whether they deserved it or not. He might even get into the car of his own accord. He wouldn't realize that anything was wrong until we got back to the hotel.

×

It was an early flight, and Guillaume's driver took us to the airport. We rode in first class, because, well, Guillaume, and there was enough privacy that Guillaume felt comfortable talking out our plans in a low voice.

"I'm thinking that when it's all over, we'll find a swamp," he said. "Wildlife should take care of the problem for us."

"Sure," I said. I was enamored with the fact that they let me order alcohol, so I wasn't paying too much attention to what he was saying. "Is our hotel this nice, too?"

"It's a nice hotel," Guillaume said.

"Soundproof?" I asked.

"Damn near," Guillaume confirmed. I'm sure Guillaume's parents, if they were still in the business of asking themselves what their son was up to, were under the impression that we were a couple. That we wanted soundproof walls so that we could have sex.

Even though I was pretty sure Guillaume was leaning that way, we had a better reason to want soundproof walls.

×

Florida was comfortable. I'd worn a T-shirt and jeans, and it was comfortable. Guillaume was in a black hoodie, as usual, and he didn't even look like he was struggling. "This is a good time to come here," I said. "When I came with the other guys, after the island, it was August and hot as balls."

"Universal's going to be busy," Guillaume said. "It's the most common time to come. Christmas through New Year's."

"Cool," I said, and Guillaume made a face. He didn't usually do good with a lot of people, or big crowds; I didn't mind them. Liked them, actually. In a crowd you could be whoever you wanted to be. In high school I went to a lot of concerts and I always stumbled out of the mosh pit bloody and grinning. If there wasn't a pit, I would start one. "Seriously. More people, more alibi."

"Sure," Guillaume said. He adjusted his grip on his backpack. We'd both packed light; backpack full of clothes and that was it. We'd buy luggage to put our souvenirs in and have more when Guillaume's driver picked us up from the airport on January 2nd.

"We've got a little over a week here," Guillaume said as we walked toward where he thought our rental car was. "It's Tuesday now. He does his livestreams on Thursdays. Today we'll check into the hotel and maybe go out to eat. Make some memories in downtown Orlando."

"What, like go clubbing?" I asked, stretching up on my toes. "You get us fake IDs?"

Guillaume nodded and I nearly fell over.

"Seriously?" I said.

"They're good," Guillaume said. "They'd fool a cop."

"That's not hard," I said, and Guillaume kicked my ankle. I grinned. "So, what clubs are we going to? Are we doing like… gay clubs?"

Guillaume looked up at me through heavy eyelids. "What makes you say that?"

"Because you're gay, right?" I said. "I mean—" This was the first time I'd brought it up since it had happened. "—if I turned you on. I'm a guy. And when we were younger... I mean, experimenting, sure, everyone does it, but—"

"I'm not anything," Guillaume said. Suddenly he seemed nervous; color was starting to rise in his cheeks and he was fidgeting with his sleeves. He shook his head. "But if you want to go to some gay clubs, Collins, we can probably make that happen."

. chapter twelve .

So the days leading up to our capture of Richard Ayers were very much a vacation. We went clubbing that first night, and Guillaume got four shots in me and then we kissed on the dance floor, with lights and sounds pounding around at the edges of our consciousness. I don't know how much he drank, if anything; all I know is that there were pictures on my phone of my tongue down his throat when I woke up the next day. When I confronted him about it, he said it was a secret we could afford to let go of if anyone questioned our time here. If we were cagey, he said, we could blame that.

Which made sense. It made sense.

I just didn't know why he thought he needed to get me drunk.

Either way, on Wednesday we had our first Universal day. I'm pretty sure that Guillaume actually had fun. Place like the Harry Potter world are so much better the more money you have, and Guillaume bought everything—Slytherin robes, the nice-quality ones, sure, but he did most of his damage in the sweets shop. Then we had to find a place to sit while he tried them all. Halfway through he got up to vomit into a trash can, and then he washed out his mouth and was right back at it.

"Happy vacation, Gill," I said when he did that, and he shot me the bird. I took a picture. I'd been taking pictures the whole time; candid stuff. Guillaume took more staged photos; for example, us in our new Slytherin robes, or outside the rides. I was posting them as I took them.

Guillaume said he was waiting for the last day, and then he'd do a photo dump. It would help with the alibi—I posted erratically, a few times a day, at different times, and Guillaume wouldn't post at all until we were back in New England and, theoretically, his pictures filled in my gaps.

We woke up early-ish on Thursday. "Let's go get breakfast at Disney," Guillaume said. We had a room with two beds, but somehow Guillaume always found his way into mine. I was fine with it. It wasn't like he took up much space. "Wander around a bit. The stream doesn't start until two, and he'll be streaming for at least an hour. It can get you some pictures."

"Sure," I said, and we headed off. I drove. Guillaume had gotten us a luxury SUV and it was similar enough to my car that I handled it all right. It was my car, just nicer. Newer. We got breakfast at a place that had the most dessert-like pancakes I'd ever seen, and I took a picture of Guillaume when he got his, which had more sprinkles on it than a toddler's birthday cake. Then we wandered a little. I took a picture of Guillaume on the *Haunted Mansion* ride, we bought a few more souvenirs, and then we were on our way to the butterfly gardens where we'd kidnap Richard Ayers.

×

The drive to the butterfly gardens was nice. It was a long stretch of two-lane highway without much traffic; we could relax. Guillaume was playing the randomest crap from my Spotify library; *Ice Nine Kills* stayed on rotation, of course, but he followed it up with shit like *Story of the Year* and *Pierce the Veil*, both of which were from my junior year emo phase. That was the year I'd gone to a lot of concerts and gotten my ass viciously beat, over and over again.

"You are such a goddam stereotype," I muttered as he moved on to *Falling in Reverse*. "Violent emo."

"This is your music, not mine," Guillaume said.

"You're choosing," I said. "You could listen to whatever you wanted. You don't have to stay in my library, but here you are, picking Ronnie Radke over… whatever else there is out there."

"Anyway, I thought that the emo stereotype was hurting yourself."

"And who's the one covered in self-harm scars?"

He did concede on that one.

×

Guillaume checked Richard's stream as we pulled up to the butterfly gardens. The gardens were old and didn't have security cameras in the parking lot, which was good. "He's saying his goodbyes," Guillaume said. "Let's go."

I turned off the car and followed him. We'd both agreed that it would be more suspicious than helpful to leave the car running—we were still running on the assumption that Richard would go with us willingly. There was one other car in the parking lot and I assumed it was his. It was a Prius.

Made sense for an environmentally conscious motherfucker like Richard Ayers.

As we got closer, I could hear Richard speaking: "And I will see you again next week! Remember to subscribe and click the notification icon so that you can get notified every time I post!"

We were on the path yet, so we weren't super suspicious when Richard, a little sweaty with a tripod over his shoulder, stumbled upon us. "Oh!" he said. "Uh, hi. Sorry if I was bothering your—Ashton?" Funny—I wasn't used to being recognized first. He made the Guillaume connection next, but he didn't pale or anything. He just looked a little confused. "Guillaume?"

"Hi," I said. "How's it going?"

"Uh, it's good," Richard said. He smiled at me, his face an easy, readable, open book. Richard Ayers had not grown much—he was taller than Guillaume, but barely. He looked like Guillaume, almost—same coloring, but Richard was tan, probably from spending his days in the Florida sun. Both had shaggy black hair and brown eyes, though Guillaume's leaned more to black. Both were slight. Narrow shoulders, narrow hips. Richard wasn't near as pretty as Guillaume, but that might have been personal preference. "I guess I sort of knew you guys were down here on vacation. I follow you on Instagram."

"Really?" I said. Even though I'd just created my account, I already had a bunch of followers and likes—something something, girls loved tragedy, something something, I had about twenty thousand of them pouring into my DMs on the daily—but I felt like I'd have recognized Richard's name, especially since we were down here for him.

"On my personal account," Richard said. "My professional account has my real name as the handle, but my personal one… it's nature, underscore, is, underscore, rich, if you wanna follow me back."

"My phone's in the car, but yeah, totally," I said. I had no intentions of following him back; I followed him already on his professional account, and adding his personal right before we killed him might point fingers in my direction. My phone was also not in the car, but I hoped that he wouldn't see, or if he saw, point out, the phone-shaped object in my pocket. "Totally, I will. Do you want to go get something to eat, or something? Catch up?"

. chapter thirteen .

Richard agreed to go with us. Of course he did. I only had to ask once, and then he was happily chattering away in the backseat of the rented SUV—convincing him to just get in the SUV had also not been difficult; we said we'd drop him back off by his car after we ate, because it was only a short drive, and he didn't need to bother with driving, and he'd even *thanked* us, saying he didn't like driving in cities or on freeways, and that he'd taken back highways to get to the butterfly gardens—while Guillaume, very judiciously, turned down the emo music.

"Where are we going?" Richard asked. "Uh, I don't mean to be a buzzkill, but I am a vegetarian. Not full vegan, but—no meat."

"That's fine," I said. I glanced at Guillaume, who grinned at me in a way that set my chest on fire. "Where do you want to go, Gill?"

"I'll find somewhere," Guillaume said. He punched the address of our hotel on my phone's GPS and set it up for me to follow, and then unbuckled and crawled into the backseat next to Richard. "Windows are tinted, Ash. Just keep driving."

I kept my eyes on the road and heard a couple of screams, but I don't know what, exactly, Guillaume did to Richard on the ride back to the hotel. I do know that he was unconscious and folded up into the massive suitcase that Guillaume had thrown in the back by the time we got there.

×

Richard was starting to stir by the time Guillaume was done tying him to the bed. "Go get us a pizza," he said to me. "Three-meat. Or as many meats as they have. Put it on the card."

I saluted him—he made a face back—and hurried off, searching up good pizza places nearby. I found one that did take-out and took a picture outside, captioning it:

GILL SICK FROM TOO MUCH CANDY… TAKE-OUT NIGHT

I posted it before going in and ordering. They were nice; let me add all their meats. I threw on some extra cheese, too, just for good measure. I figured I might as well make it good. Was Guillaume definitely going to force-feed Richard Ayers meat just because he'd said he was a vegetarian? Absolutely.

But I got an extra-large, so there'd be some for me, too, and it smelled great. I chatted with the guys behind the counter while the pizza was being made. I was a little antsy to get back, but there was also something electric in the anticipation. What the hell would Ayers look like when I got back?

×

The answer was 'bad.'

I probably could have guessed that much.

×

I balanced the pizza on one arm (I had a couple bottles of soda under the other; Coke for me, crème soda for

Guillaume) and opened up the door. I shut it behind me, set down the pizza and the pop, and put on the deadbolt and chain before turning around and witnessing everything.

Guillaume had duct tape over Richard's mouth; a screamer, then. Tears and blood streaked Richard's face; he looked absolutely bewildered that this was happening; bewildered and pained. His one arm was handcuffed to the bed. The other was at an angle it shouldn't have been.

"Ash," Guillaume said.

"Gill," I said. I tossed him the crème soda. "Got the pizza. Man, it looks good. I'm eating some before we get started."

"You got a big one, right?" Guillaume said. He tugged at Richard's hair and Richard shuddered, flinching away from him. "We need to feed our guest. God, this was a good idea. We hardly got to play with Spence at all."

"You're creepy," I said. "C'mon, let's eat before this gets cold."

So we ate, sitting on the bed across from Richard, watching him for some time, until I got bored and turned on the TV. The best part about vacationing with Guillaume was that he would buy all the movies you could want, so I was able to find a *Saw* film and start that going. "Did we watch these?" I asked Guillaume.

"Not all of them," Guillaume said. "They started getting dumb. Plot-wise, I mean."

"Are you telling me that *you* aren't watching them for the kills?" I said. "I watch them for the kills. That's the *best part* of a *Saw* movie."

"I guess," Guillaume said. "But if something's trying to be smart, maybe it should be, I dunno, actually smart."

Richard made a muffled sound under his duct tape and Guillaume grabbed the TV remote from me and whipped it at him. It hit him in the chest with a *smack* and he flinched. Fresh tears started making tracks down his cheeks.

"It's a good idea to watch a movie like this, anyway," Guillaume said. "For the screaming."

"Right," I said. I wasn't sure if anyone would buy that screams from *Saw* and screams from Richard Ayers were the same, but Guillaume stood to jack up the volume on the TV, so I figured it might work. Sort of.

Then he went to Richard, who was shaking as he flinched away, pressing his face into his shoulder, the one attached to the hand that was cuffed to the bedframe, and Guillaume tore the duct tape off of his mouth. Richard yelped. "Guillaume, please, please—" he begged. "Please, please don't, it's okay, it's okay, I never—I'd never—"

"This is mostly why I taped his mouth," Guillaume said. "Shit gets old after a while. You hungry, Ayers?"

"I—I—no, not really—um—"

"Ash, pizza," Guillaume said, and I brought over what was left of the pizza. It was starting to get cold, and the cheese was starting to congeal. I wasn't sure how Richard was going to eat it without gagging, but maybe that was the point. Guillaume could beat Richard up all day long, sure, but he'd like to be creative.

Guillaume was creative.

"Open," Guillaume said. Richard shook his head, his jaw clenched, and then Guillaume leaned on his broken arm and Richard got real pale, real fast, and looked about two seconds away from passing out. "*O-pen.*"

Richard opened.

Guillaume shoved the pizza in his mouth, so fast and so deep that Richard gagged. Guillaume didn't let him spit it out—the kid was going to choke to death, I figured—just held it there, shoving more in. Richard chewed and swallowed furiously, but I saw his throat convulse a few times by the time Guillaume tossed the crust to the floor. Richard, as soon as his mouth was clear, coughed long and hard. "*Please*," he gasped. "Please, I'll eat it, you don't have to, I don't, I can't—"

Guillaume shoved another piece of pizza in his mouth. Richard gagged again. It went on like this, for two more pieces, before Richard started whipping his head around, trying to avoid it. "I'm gonna *puke*, Guillaume, *seriously*—"

"You puke, and you're licking it up," Guillaume said, and then grabbed him by the jaw and shoved another piece of pizza in. He was totally focused in on this kid. I shifted from foot-to-foot, honestly, a little bored. Sure, there was a part of me that was whispering at the back of my head, telling me that this was sick, this was wrong, Richard Ayers had done *nothing* fucking wrong—Ryan Spencer maybe hadn't deserved to *die*, but at least he'd been an asshole. Richard Ayers hadn't even testified against Guillaume at the trial. He'd been so out of it on the island that he just didn't have anything to say.

A bigger part of me was bored because Guillaume didn't really need help with this one.

Richard was heaving, now, whenever Guillaume gave him space to breathe. Guillaume glanced back at me. "We should have put the tarp down under him before we started."

"I can hold him off the bed while you get it down," I said, crossing over to them and picking Richard up princess-style. Richard Ayers was light. Guillaume nodded and went digging around for the tarp, which we'd bought with cash at a Wal-Mart a few days ago. We'd bought a bunch of less-creepy stuff alongside it that implied camping more than murder; tents and swimsuits and whatnot.

Guillaume spread the tarp out and I dropped Richard, who moaned when his broken arm hit the bed first. "Sorry," I said.

Guillaume snorted. "We're about to *kill* this kid and you're apologizing to him?"

"K—Guillaume, please, please, please—"

Guillaume backhanded him, not really even looking at him, and Richard devolved back into quiet sobs and shaking. "What?" I said. "I'm a nice guy."

"I know," Guillaume said.

. chapter fourteen .

Guillaume went to bed early. We figured that he'd sleep from nine to two, and then I'd take two to seven, and then we'd kill Richard and finish up our vacation. We were going to dump his body in some swamp and let the alligators eat him. It seemed reasonable. Richard was not sleeping. He was crying and trying to pull his one wrist free. He'd bled freely on the tarp. I was glad we'd put it down.

    I was watching *28 Days Later* on TV. It was pretty good.

    "Ashton," I heard, from Richard's direction, and glanced over my shoulder at him.

    "What?"

    "Why are you—why—you're not—" Richard was stumbling over his words, which I *got*, really; he was hurting, bleeding out, probably, broken bones. He should've been trying to get as comfortable as he could right now, really, before it was Guillaume's turn. I wasn't really interested in hurting people without Guillaume there, conscious and next to me, but he didn't need me to hurt someone.

    Not like I needed him.

    "I'm not what?" I asked.

    Richard's mouth opened and closed a few times, but nothing came out.

    "Not like him?" I said. "Not a sadist? Not a monster? Not a psychopath? Richie, I know you weren't exactly *around* a lot on the island, but you gotta remember that we were Siamese twins back then, too, right?"

Richard was quiet.

"You could let me go," he said, his voice quiet. Breaking. "I—I didn't—I didn't do anything to either of you. I didn't even testify against him. Like you did."

"I know," I said. "We've gotten over it."

Richard's chin trembled wildly.

"You can keep crying," I said. "I don't care, and I think he likes it."

Then I turned back to my movie.

×

When I woke up, Richard was nearly dead. He was bleeding out, a gaping hole in his stomach. Guillaume was wrist-deep in innards. "Jesus, Gill," I muttered. "What a way to start the morning."

"You're up late," Guillaume said. It was seven-fifteen.

"I thought I set an alarm," I said. I pushed myself up to sit. Richard's eyes weren't seeing much of anything anymore; that searching, pleading look they'd had last night was gone. Now they were just staring blankly as he made little hiccup-y noises and bled. "Is clean-up gonna take all morning, then?"

. chapter fifteen .

"We'll weigh down this shit," Guillaume said. "Sink it. And dump his naked body in the swamp and let the alligators eat him."

"Awesome," I said. "Is the swamp near? Because I think this car you rented is going to stink like dead bodies for the next thirty years."

"Yeah," Guillaume said. "Turn here."

Guillaume was buzzing in a way he hadn't after we'd killed Ryan Spencer. Maybe it was because Ryan's death had been so short; it had been a brief fight and then one slice and it was done. Richard Ayers had lasted hours. Probably he'd begged at the end. I didn't know. I'd been asleep.

Today, we were going to dump Richard's body and then head to Disney. We'd hang out there all day, and then spend a couple more days just soaking in Orlando. Maybe we'd find our way to some more clubs. Guillaume hadn't kissed me since that first night and it was slowly driving me crazy. Given his general attitude, I wouldn't thought he'd be insatiable after killing Richard Ayers.

But he wasn't, and so I had to make do without him.

×

It was sticky, and hot, and deserted. I'd followed Guillaume's instructions until we were deep in the swamp, on a dirt road that was hardly a road, and we only stopped because I was pretty sure the road was just turning into more swamp.

"This has got to be far enough," I said. I pulled my T-shirt away from my chest in a weak attempt to stop feeling like I was strangling. The heat was absolutely oppressive. I'd never wished for a white Christmas more than in that moment.

"Probably," Guillaume admitted. He opened up the hatchback. "Help me with this."

I helped him pull the suitcase out of the back of the SUV and unzipped it. The smell of Richard, of blood and shit and the beginning of bloat, probably accelerated by the heat (even though I'd been blasting the AC), hit me and I had to bite down hard on my tongue in an attempt to stop myself from gagging.

"So, what," I said, my voice shaky. We hadn't had to deal with Ryan Spencer's body. We'd just left it. "What, we just… dump him in?"

"And then fill the suitcase with the tarps and some rocks and toss it in after him," Guillaume said. He crouched down. "Tip it."

"What?"

"*Tip* it. How the fuck can you be so ready to kill a guy and not to deal with the clean-up?"

I shook my head. I felt lightheaded, a little, but I crouched and tipped it. Guillaume guided Richard's body into the water with a soft *splash*. "Okay, question two," I said. "Where are we going to… what are we going to fill this with, again?"

"Heavy shit," Guillaume said. He seemed irritated; I don't know if he was nervous, but I sure as fuck was. There was something so much more *final* about disposing of a body. Killing Ryan Spencer had been over like *that*;

Richard Ayers felt like it was taking years. "Rocks. Branches. Whatever."

"Okay," I said. I scrounged around, one eye out for alligators. Giant heavy rocks were hard to find in the swamp, but I came up with enough to weigh the suitcase down, at the very least. "Can you help me throw it in? I know I'm the brawn of the operation, Gill, but this shit's *heavy*."

Guillaume grumbled, but he helped.

Then we went and finished up our vacation.

. chapter sixteen .

I was nervous about the rest of our vacation, to tell you the truth. We were very publicly in Florida, and Richard Ayers had just disappeared in Florida... but nobody approached us. This was probably major police oversight. Guillaume was a well-known psychopath, a well-known killer, and there he was, walking down the streets at theme parks without a care in the world. I think our, or more likely, *his*, attitudes helped us out there. I was a little jumpy.

    Guillaume was fine.

    My problem, I think, is that I am and always have been an overthinker. When I'm in the moment, I'm good. I've got that shit. I can kill a man, I can help Guillaume kill a man, whatever has to be done. But when it's over and I think about the *consequences*—that's when shit really goes sideways.

    For me, at least.

×

Our second semester of college started out normal enough. Getting used to new classes, new professors, new study groups—it was almost enough to make me think I was normal for a few weeks. The only difference in terms of classload this semester was that I had a class with Guillaume.

    Math 102. It was a general. It shocked me, a little, that Guillaume didn't have all of his generals taken care of, but he'd never been one for math or science and so I guess, maybe, I shouldn't have been shocked. We sat together, in the back corner away from the door, and I tried to pay attention while Guillaume tried to pass me notes about which of our erstwhile classmates he wanted to kill next. I kept pushing them back without reading them and he got so irritated he stabbed himself in the hand with a pencil.

"*Shit, Gill!*"

I yelled loud enough to stop the professor, who was about eighty and droned on no matter what was going on, stopped talking. "Mr...?"

"Collins," I said. "Um, I'm sorry, I need to—I'm sorry."

I shoved my stuff into my bag and Guillaume's stuff into his bag and then grabbed him by the arm and hoisted him up and out and dragged him out into the hallway. The droning continued behind us. "*Gill*," I said. "What the fuck?"

"You weren't paying attention to me," Guillaume said. "Voila."

He extended his hand. The pencil hadn't gone all the way through, thank the fucking lord, but it was in deep enough that it was standing, straight up-and-down. My stomach lurched. I don't know why I was able to handle Richard Ayers mutilated on a hotel bed behind me but one pencil in Guillaume's hand made me feel like I was about to puke. Maybe it was because I liked Guillaume.

"Jesus," I muttered. "Should we—"

"I don't need the hospital," Guillaume said. He held onto his wrist with his other hand and then, before I could do anything to stop him, took the eraser between his teeth and pulled the pencil out. He ripped it out, quickly, before I could stop him, and then he spat it onto the floor. The hole in his hand was a perfect circle, a few centimeters deep, and oozing. I felt my stomach lurch again.

"Let me at least put some like… I dunno, some peroxide on that or something," I said. My voice was weak. I kept looking at the pencil on the floor. It was a standard pencil, a number two Ticonderoga, and the blood from Guillaume's hand had stained the yellow and there was blood dripping from the point, which wasn't even that sharp. I wondered if it had broken off in Guillaume's hand or if he'd just used that much force.

I didn't want to know.

"Okay," Guillaume said. He bent to pick up the pencil and then sucked the blood off the tip before sticking it into a side pocket of his backpack. Some of it escaped his mouth and stained the corner of his lips red. I had to tear my eyes away from it.

Sometimes I think I'm just as fucked up as Guillaume is.

×

Our next victim would be Victor Walsh.

Guillaume announced this to me that same day, when we were back in our dorm and getting ready for bed. Well, when I was getting ready for bed—Guillaume would stay up until two or three in the morning reading. He used the lamp at the desk and it wasn't irritating, not really; I could handle it. Honestly, the little 'annoying roommate' things Guillaume did didn't bother me at all. He could be killing animals, so I figured things like him leaving moldy pints of ice cream around and reading late into the night were the least of my worries.

"Walsh?" I said. "I thought you wanted to stay away from the athletic ones?"

Vic Walsh had been one of our crew. He'd played football, he'd been relatively speedy, but more than that, he had these big broad shoulders that everyone *knew* would turn him into someone big and hard to mess with one day.

"He's not athletic anymore," Guillaume said. "He's all spindly. Broad-shouldered still, he can't get away from his bones, but he doesn't work out. And he's always been too nice for his own good."

That was true. While people like Ryan Spencer were assholes, and I'd been willing to follow along with just about anything, Vic Walsh had some kind of moral code that actually made me wonder how he'd gotten back from the island alive.

"All he does now," Guillaume said, standing up from his desk and throwing a printout of some pictures on my desk. "Is play video games. He games all day, all night; he doesn't even go to college. He *Twitch streams*."

"He's a Twitch streamer?" I said.

"You know what that is?"

"Yeah, well, not all of us have been in the psych ward for the past six years, Gill."

Guillaume stared at me, and if I hadn't known him well I would've thought he was pissed. But he wasn't. He was just waiting for me to explain what a Twitch streamer was. So I did, and he snorted and thought it was a waste of time (and, well, he was probably right) and then we went back to planning.

"The only problem with Walsh," Guillaume said, biting down hard on a popsicle—the minifridge had an actual, decent freezer, because, again, Guillaume was richer than God—and letting it melt in his mouth for a second or two before swallowing. "Is that he's *streaming* like fourteen hours a day. And if he's not on at the time he normally is, his *fans* will get weirded out, because for some goddam reason, there are about a *million of them* waiting to watch him play—whatever he plays."

I nodded. "So it'll have to be fast."

"The good news," Guillaume said. "Is that he makes enough money from this and it's apparently annoying enough to his family that he does have an apartment. We won't have to dodge parents."

"But it'll still have to be fast."

"Yeah," Guillaume said. He didn't sound too put out by it, though. I think the idea of the challenge really appealed to him, to be completely honest. Ryan Spencer'd had a time crunch, sure, but if push came to shove, we could've killed his entire family. We couldn't kill the million people who liked to watch Vic Walsh play video games. "Unless we kill him live."

. chapter seventeen .

In the realm of Guillaume's 'terrible ideas that were going to get us thrown in prison,' killing Vic Walsh live as he was streaming whatever shitty video game he was currently streaming was up there. Up there higher than kidnapping Richard Ayers *after* a stream—I wondered, briefly, what memo I'd missed, if we were all making money *streaming* nowadays—and higher than killing Ryan Spencer while his family was on a picnic.
 "We're going to get caught," I said.
 "We'll wear masks," Guillaume said.
 "But—"
 "He lives alone, Ash," Guillaume said. "*And* he already soundproofed his place for us, because he yells all the time. I looked it up. Streamers do that."
 "How do you know he did?"
 "I asked him," Guillaume said. Seeing the look on my face, he grinned, let me think that he'd already given Vic hints that he was about to come and kill him, and then explained. "In an anonymous comment while he was streaming. I asked if he soundproofed his apartment because of all of the yelling he does while he's playing video games. Honestly, even if some noise does break through, his neighbors are used to him being loud and annoying as shit."
 "Okay," I said. Despite the fact that 'murdering someone live on camera' was still something that weirded me out like, on the legal level, it was starting to feel a little

better. I started to think that we could actually do this. "Where does he live?"

That's where the next issue came in.

"Minnesota."

×

It would take another long weekend to do this shit, and Guillaume was trying to convince me to make it spring break. "My parents want me home," I said.

"Yeah, well, I've never been to the Mall of America," Guillaume said. "We fly to Minneapolis. We rent a car. Walsh lives in Monticello; it's about forty miles north. We hit the Mall of America, and… and maybe a hockey game or something."

"Gill, do you even care about hockey?"

"Out of all of the sports, it is the least boring," Guillaume said. I should've figured. Trust Guillaume to only like the most violent sport, where fighting is not only tolerated but almost a part of the game.

I played a year of hockey in high school.

High school hockey doesn't really let you hurt people, though. Everyone's all concerned about concussions and won't let you throw punches like they do in the NHL. But you can still slam people into the boards and stuff. That's how you play the game.

"My mom's going to realize something's up," I said. "If we keep going on vacations to these places—you know, these places close to where we have former classmates who, oops, *keep turning up dead*."

"They haven't found Ayers," Guillaume said. "He's probably in an alligator's stomach by now."

"But he disappeared," I said.

"But if we kidnapped him, obviously someone would have figured it out by now," Guillaume said. "Chill, Ash. Besides, your mom wants to believe that you're better now."

"I didn't need to get better," I said. "That was just you."

"Was it?" Guillaume asked, and it hit me, some kind of deep, squirming feeling in the pit of my stomach. Guillaume was nuts, evil, whatever you wanted to call it—I was the normal one. Fuck if I was anything worse than a *follower*. I did what Gill told me to do.

That was it. Nothing worse than that.

. chapter eighteen .

"Ashton, I really wish you'd come *home*," my mom said on the other side of the phone, like I knew she would. "You could bring Guillaume here."

"Maybe Easter," I said, even though I was pretty sure we'd be off killing Zach Blanchard or Leo Moore or Steven Murphy by then. Guillaume was determined to take advantage of all of these breaks we had.

"Well, Easter…" Mom trailed off. "We like to have family for Easter."

"So? Gill's practically family," I said. I was eating a bag of Dorito's in bed and Guillaume was reading on the bed across the way, and he gave me an amused look. "He's been over for holidays before."

"Well, that was before…" Mom trailed off again. "I mean, your cousins? Around him?"

"They wouldn't have let him out if he wasn't better, Mom," I said. I crunched a few more Dorito's. Guillaume was watching me, so I sucked the Dorito dust off of my middle finger and flipped him off. "He won't *hurt* anyone."

"They might not want to come," Mom said.

"So?" I said. "You're always complaining about having to order in so much food. If a couple cousins don't come, that's fine. I'd rather spend time with Gill. He's got so much catching up to do when it comes to like, regular life."

Cousins didn't like coming over to our house, anyway. We had acres of trees and someone always got hurt. They'd fall off a high branch or they'd step on a rusty nail or something; it wasn't like living out in the country was all that safe. Guillaume, even, one of the few times he'd come over before the island, had stepped on the tine of a rusty pitchfork and we'd had to take him to the emergency room. They'd shot him up with a tetanus vaccine and his parents had sent mine a check covering the visit and then some—a convenience fee, Guillaume had called it.

Mom sighed. "We didn't even get to see you over Christmas. It looked like you had a good time in Florida."

"We did," I said.

The line was quiet. Guillaume still had his book out, but he was pretty clearly tracking me with his eyes instead of looking at the words.

"Easter," Mom said, finally. "I'm holding you to that. Bring Guillaume if you have to."

"Will do," I said, and then there was a beep and the call was over. "She's pissed at me because you keep dragging me around the continental United States to kill people and she never sees me anymore."

"Ash, did your parents pay that much attention to you when you lived with them?" Guillaume asked.

"More than yours did."

"That's not hard to do," Guillaume said. He stretched, like a cat, and tossed his book across the room. It landed face-up. It was *You've Lost a Lot of Blood* by Eric LaRocca. I'd never heard of it, but from the cover, it sure looked like Guillaume's kind of book. "But mine kept me supervised with nannies."

"I would've thought they'd get an *au pair* for you," I said, only half-joking.

"Oh, they did," Guillaume said. "I just didn't want to confuse you with French."

I considered, then balled up what was left of my chips in the bag and tossed it at him. The bag hit him in the forehead and he glared at me. I grinned at him. If I hadn't been so secure in my, at the very least *semi*-importance to Guillaume, I would have been scared by that glare. But I did know that even if Guillaume wanted to hurt me, he didn't want to hurt me to death.

He wanted to keep me around.

×

It was snowing in Minnesota when we landed. Not hard, and they were the big, fluffy flakes that spoke of warm weather, but it was snowing. I nearly ate shit right there on the tarmac, and Guillaume watched me with some amusement.

"I'm not good at winter driving," I said, shivering a little. I'd worn a sweatshirt, but what was fine back in Connecticut was not fine in Minnesota. "Are you sure we have to rent a car?"

"I can winter drive if you won't," Guillaume said. "I'm not scared."

"Maybe that's worse," I said. "At least I *have* driven in winter before."

Guillaume muttered, but he followed me to where our car was—it was, at the very least, an SUV again—and I took us through the snowy streets of Minneapolis to our hotel. The city was warm enough that the roads were more slushy than anything, but my knuckles were white as I drove.

It was fine, though.

We were staying at the hotel attached to the Mall of America, and this time we only had one bed. "What, you decide to stop pretending?" I asked, and Guillaume elbowed me in the diaphragm and I had to spend a couple of minutes coughing.

. chapter nineteen .

We spent a few days at the mall, buying shit, eating at every food place in the building—the ones that were mostly sugar twice or three times—and spending money. Just like Universal, the Mall of America was a lot more fun when you had the cash to throw around. Guillaume dropped a small fortune in *Sugar Rush*, and then another small fortune in *Hot Topic*, which I found hilarious.

"God, it is so sad that you never got to have a real emo phase," I said as Guillaume put on his new *My Chemical Romance* T-shirt. "If only the psych ward would've let you go to concerts."

"We can go to concerts this summer," Guillaume said. "I don't really care about the music. I just like the design."

"Of course you do," I said. He looked good, to be fair, in the big clunky black cargo pants and chains and emo band T-shirts. With his hair in his face and the scars that littered everywhere he could, probably, touch… it matched. It looked good. Guillaume has always been better-looking than me; I've always looked relatively normal. Average. Brown hair, average height, maybe a little on the tall end, kind of broad but nothing exceptional.

Guillaume—he was exceptional.

"Make a list of shows you want to go to," Guillaume said. "After school lets out. Maybe one of them will take us near someone fun."

'Someone fun,' if you haven't caught on, means 'someone we can kill.'

"If you really think we'll be able to keep it up that long," I said. "Honestly, I think it's a miracle we haven't been caught already. After Walsh…" I trailed off.

"We haven't been caught already because the police are stupid," Guillaume said. "And they don't share information with each other. Florida and Minnesota are so far apart."

"This one's going to be risky," I said. "And we might get caught."

Guillaume shrugged. "I won't tell about the other ones if you don't," he said. "We don't want to get extradited to Florida. They have the death penalty."

"And Minnesota doesn't?"

Guillaume shook his head. "The upper Midwest is actually pretty anti-death penalty," he said. "Our safe states are North Dakota, Minnesota, Michigan, Illinois, Iowa, Wisconsin, Alaska, Hawaii, Washington, Colorado, New Mexico, West Virginia, regular Virginia, Maryland, Delaware, New Jersey, Connecticut, Rhode Island, New York, Massachusetts, Vermont, New Hampshire, and Maine."

"Safe states," I muttered.

"Well, relatively safe," Guillaume said. "Also, I have a history of psychotic breaks that result in violence, so I might just go back to the nuthouse."

"Take me with you," I said. "The nuthouse you were at seemed nice."

"It was nice," Guillaume said. He considered, and then added, "But a gilded cage is still a cage."

×

We got on the road to Monticello early one morning when it was supposed to be clear and the roads were supposed to be good. That didn't mean I was prepared to drive for forty minutes on the interstate. Luckily, since it *was* March, the roads had a chance of being decent.

And they were decent. I was just freaking out.

We stopped at KFC for lunch and Guillaume ate more real food than I'd ever seen him eat before in my life. Normally the guy would swallow sugar by the bucketful, but anything with like, protein in it, unless that protein was from a peanut butter in a Reese's cup, was picked at at best.

But he was swallowing a whole lot of chicken for sure.

"Hungry?" I said.

"Yeah," Guillaume said. He washed it all down with some new Mountain Dew flavor.

Then we went out to find Vic Walsh.

×

Guillaume had, of course, tracked down his address. I wondered what kind of second-party person he was having track these people down and how long it would take for that person to act on the fact that they *had* to know what Guillaume was doing. There was no way that they didn't catch on to the fact that every time Guillaume asked them for an address, that person ended up dead.

×

Vic Walsh was in a nice apartment. Like I've said, most of us who crashed on the island had money, and those of us that survived made more. It's amazing the kind of money people will throw at you when you're in a tragedy. All you have to do is post one of those GoFundMe's and say that you need help and people will just pump money in like you'll die if they don't. As well as that, the *novelty* of it made the people that decided to make their money online, like Richard Ayers and Vic Walsh, have an almost built-in audience.

"How do we get in?" I asked.

"We buzz in," Guillaume said.

"How do we buzz in when we don't know anyone here?"

"Oh, sorry," Guillaume said. "You buzz in, Ashton. He'll let you in."

"How d'you know that?"

"Because you're the likable one," Guillaume said. "He'll buy you wanting to come and see him. He'll know I want to kill him."

I sighed and pressed the buzzer that said 'WALSH.'

There was a brief moment of silence, and then, from the other side: "Hello?"

"Um—" I said. "It's Ashton. From school."

"You are going to have to be more specific than that, chief," the voice on the other side said.

"Middle school," I said. "Ashton Collins."

It was silent for another moment.

"Like… middle school… crashed on an island… everything went crazy… Guillaume Argot… that Ashton Collins?"

"The one and only," I said. Guillaume rolled his eyes at me and I kicked him. "Listen, can I come up? It's cold out here. I don't know why you live here."

"Why?" he said.

"Um," I said. "Because it's cold out here?"

"I mean, why are you here? I follow you on Instagram, Ash," he said. "I know Guillaume's with you. Cut the crap. He's out there with you, isn't he?"

It might have been my imagination, but he sounded scared.

Guillaume pushed me aside and took over. When he spoke, I saw the kid who had fooled a dozen psychologists into letting him out of the 'nut house,' as he'd so succinctly put it. "I'm out here, Vic," he said. "We were in Minneapolis for spring break and noticed you lived nearby. We just want to visit."

"Then why did Ashton let me think that it was just him out here?"

"Because we figured you'd think I was still crazy," Guillaume said. "I'm not. They wouldn't have let me out if I was. I've been in college and haven't even drawn blood on anyone other than myself, I promise."

It was quiet.

"C'mon," I said. "We were in town for the mall and a hockey game and you were close enough for a visit. We haven't seen anyone else since we were little. Let us up."

Silence.

Finally, a sigh. "Whatever," he said.

Click.

We were in.

. chapter twenty .

Guillaume was almost giddy as we tripped our way up to Vic Walsh's apartment. I don't think he actually believed that would get us in, or something, because he was practically skipping. It was unnerving. "You gotta calm down," I said as we rounded the last turn of the stairs. "If he lets us in and he sees you this happy he's going to know something's up."

"Or he'll think they have me on some real heavy-duty shit," Guillaume said, but he did calm down.

Vic was waiting for us in the hallway, leaning against his door, arms folded. "Hi," he said cautiously.

"Hey, Vic," I said. "Can we... come in?"

"I guess," Vic said, and he opened the door and he let us in.

Vic Walsh's apartment was overflowing with video game and anime merchandise. He didn't really look the part of the stereotypical video game nerd; he was skinny, but I was pretty sure that was because he didn't eat. Like I've said, some of us ate like crazy after the island and some of us didn't eat at all. Vic was the latter. I looked him up, after Guillaume had figured out he was a *streamer*, and there were people online who were worried about him having an eating disorder because he streamed for so long and didn't take a bite once.

I could've told them that it wasn't a regular eating disorder, it was just the fact that he couldn't stand meat after cannibalizing Callum Reid. Or maybe any food at all. Maybe he didn't think he *deserved* it; Vic had been another guy who'd had a pretty big hand in Sage Horton's death, just like Ryan Spencer, and Sage Horton had had the gnarliest death on the island.

Probably if Vic every ate anything, it was the bare minimum and ultra-processed like Cheetos.

Vic sat down in an armchair and gestured toward the couch. "Sit," he said. "Why not. You're here to kill me, right?"

Guillaume froze. I laughed.

"Jeez, Vic," I said. "Dramatic, huh?"

"Why else would you be here?" Vic said. "I mean, Ryan and Richard died when Guillaume got out. I figure you go to college somewhere close to Ryan and I saw your guys' Instagram posts down in Florida when Richard went missing. So when I saw you were up here I figured it was my turn."

"We're here to see a hockey game," Guillaume said.

"Oh, sure," Vic said. "I'm sure you just have a burning passion for the *Minnesota Wild.* You know, there are about ten better NHL teams you could've gone to see much closer to where you guys are based. I'm sure."

"Mall, too," Guillaume said.

"Gill loves that Hot Topic," I said. "I'd laugh if it wasn't so stereotypical."

Guillaume kicked me and I grinned again.

"Do you *want* to die or something?" I asked. Amazingly—and I was kind of enjoying it—Guillaume was shaken. He wasn't expecting Vic to come at him like this, and honestly, neither was I. Vic had been a follower, sure, he'd played football with the rest of us, but he'd also been positive. He'd been relatively nice.

He hadn't been sarcastic. He hadn't been like *this*.

Vic shrugged. "Sometimes I feel like I'm wasting borrowed time, anyway," he said. "I mean, what am I even doing? *Streaming video games*? That's my fucking *job*. It's such a waste of time. All of this is such a waste of time."

"Let's go," Guillaume said.

"What?"

"This isn't fun if he wants to die," he said.

"Gill, if he—he could tell someone, you know that, right?" I said.

"If you want to get rid of him, do it," Guillaume said. "I'll be in the car."

×

I did, at the very least, kill him quick.

. chapter twenty-one .

The hockey game was fun. I hadn't gone to a hockey game since I'd played, and even those—they did try really hard to make sure that high school kids didn't actually slaughter each other. Adults, in the NHL, they were allowed to slaughter each other, and that was fun. Guillaume enjoyed it too, I think… at the very least, he enjoyed the concessions stands. You have not lived until you've paid roughly two hundred dollars for food at a professional sports game.

But we headed back to college on Sunday. The news on Vic Walsh hadn't broken yet. I hadn't hidden his body or anything, but I guess he didn't have too many IRL friends. Probably some of his fans were calling the police and stuff, but fans calling the police were probably not near as effective as friends or family.

"Who's next?" I asked Guillaume as we unpacked our bags back in our dorm room. It was wonderful to go from Minnesota, where it was still cold in March, to our little New England college, which was, at the very least, recognizably spring.

Guillaume didn't answer for a while, and when I looked at him, I expected him to be studying his list. He kept it on him at all times, in his wallet, I think, and it was starting to get crumpled and stained. But he wasn't. He was looking at me.

"What?" I said.

"You killed Vic Walsh," he said.

"Yeah," I said. "It had to be done. Don't tell me you're getting soft on—"

Guillaume lunged, and I almost ducked out of the way before I realized he wasn't trying to hurt me. He wrapped his arms around my neck and forced me back onto my bed and he kissed me, hard. It seemed that the only thing that turned him on to me more than me getting hurt was me hurting someone else.

"Ashton Collins, you are fucking perfect," Guillaume breathed into my ear. "You were *made for me*."

"Sure, Gill," I managed back. He was gripping my face like if he let up for a second I'd disappear. I wasn't sure how much experience Guillaume had, in the carnal matters, but I figured, unless there was abuse going on in that fancy asylum of his, it was mostly just what he'd done with me. Both now and when we were kids. Not that we got into too much when we were kids, but we did a little experimenting between the horror movies and torturing of small animals. Your regular preteen 'I'm bored and kind of interested in this' stuff. You know how it is.

"You have everyone fooled," Guillaume said. He kissed me again and bit my lip so hard we could both taste my blood. "You're just like me, but you fooled everyone."

"We can't all be the lord of darkness, man," I said. "Some of us have to be normal."

"Ash," Guillaume said. "You are the farthest thing from normal.

×

Our next victim was going to be Nicky Wilder.

Both of us kind of wanted to go after Kevin, you know, because as the real villain he should've been the one locked up instead of Guillaume, but there was no way we were getting near him. Guillaume had looked into it. The guy had around the clock security. Not as protection against Guillaume, because Guillaume was, according to the courts and the professionals, cured, but as protection against any crazies that might want to take justice into their own hands.

Don't get me wrong. Guillaume probably deserved more than he'd gotten.

But Kevin deserved some of it, too. Guillaume was the enforcer, but Kevin was the *leader*. Nobody would've followed along with what Guillaume was doing if Kevin hadn't. Guillaume just wasn't that popular. If Kevin hadn't gone along with what Guillaume was doing, it would've been me and Guillaume on a tiny corner of that island grabbing whoever came near.

But Kevin was out of the question.

So Nicky Wilder.

Nicky Wilder was, to my best recollection, sort of a loser. He'd blossomed, a little, on the island, but when we'd crashed he'd been like, a boy scout, and when we looked him up, we discovered that he'd turned into a protein-guzzling monster.

Guillaume and I, not so much.

"We'll have to take him by surprise," Guillaume said when I pointed this out. "We can take a gun or something."

"I thought you didn't like guns," I said.

"I don't," Guillaume said. "I like get more up close and personal. But they're good for a threat."

I acquiesced, and we went back to planning.

"So, what," I said. "We threaten him with a gun and then… tie him up, or something? I can't hold him down while you cut him up, he's too big."

"I know that," Guillaume said. He bit down hard on his thumbnail. "I want to do a hard one, though, before we go after Kevin or Adam. I really want to get either Kevin or Adam, but when we do, it's all going to go tits up. You know that, right? That when we go to the big ones…"

"Someone's going to realize that we've been systematically killing off our former classmates that we were stranded on an island with five years ago?" I said. "Yeah. I think it's amazing that they haven't already, to be honest."

"I'm sure someone has," Guillaume said. "I'm sure someone has put together that I'm out and we're together and they're dying. But I'm also sure that people are brushing it off as some kind of conspiracy theory. Kids killing kids on a deserted island is one thing. Adults who are semi- in the public eye going after people is another. It's harder to believe because…" He groped for words, and then shook his head. "You just don't want to believe it."

×

But before Nicky Wilder, we had Easter.

×

My mother was not pleased when I said that I was going through with bringing Guillaume home for Easter.

"I thought that maybe he would have something better to do," she said. "His family must want to see him."

"Honestly, Mom, I don't think they do," I said. "Did you tell the cousins he was coming?"

The silence was enough.

"Well, they'll get a surprise, then," I said.

She sighed, and I could practically hear her disappointment over the phone. If I closed my eyes, she was right in front of me, her arms crossed, her eyes to the sky as she wisher her only son was not the best friend of a convicted psychotic murderer.

She hung up, then, and I tossed my phone onto my bed. "She's not too happy," I told Guillaume.

"Did you think she would be?" he said. He was stretched across his bed, catlike, reading a book, *The Bone Season* by Samantha Shannon. He seemed vaguely bored by this one; unlike most people, when Guillaume didn't like a book, he read it as fast as he possibly could so that he could be done with it. He didn't believe in giving up—he liked to finish what he started.

"I thought she'd at least pretend a little more," I admitted.

"Maybe she's putting it all together," Guillaume suggested. He dog-eared his page and tossed the book onto the floor before sitting up. "Can we go to Dairy Queen? They have new blizzard flavors."

. chapter twenty-two .

"Your house hasn't changed," Guillaume said as we drove up.

"Why would it?" I said. "My parents didn't need to move into the hills because of their only son's actions, you know."

Guillaume's family (and Kevin's) had sold their mansions for more remote mansions. As far as I knew, from what Guillaume had said, his parents lived up in the mountains now. I was sure it was some kind of giant mountain cabin retreat situation, but they had moved. His old neighbors had not been super delighted about living next to murder parents.

"Oh, right," Guillaume said. "Their only son's actions stayed under wraps."

"Exactly," I said. I didn't see anyone else's car yet, so either we were early or Mom had caved and told everyone I was bringing Guillaume and they weren't coming. "Did your parents care when you told them you weren't coming home for Easter?"

"I didn't," Guillaume said. "They're figuring we're on another trip."

"How do you know that if you didn't talk to them?"

"Because this morning my dad transferred a couple thousand dollars into my checking account," Guillaume said. "He does that when we go on trips. If I texted him and said we were doing Europe, he'd send back a thumbs up emoji and then transfer me more money."

"Jesus, you've got it made," I muttered.

Guillaume shrugged. "It works for us," he said. "You know, as a family."

"Sure," I said. "As a family."

I parked and got out. We'd both packed light, because we were only going to be here a couple of days, and I grabbed Guillaume's backpack as well as mine. Most of the kids who had crashed on the island had moved. Even if they weren't chased out by angry neighbors worried they would slaughter their children, they had scattered to the four winds. That's why we'd found Richard Ayers in Florida and Vic Walsh in Minnesota.

But we'd stayed. Guillaume recognized the house.

"Nothing here's changed," he said, but his voice was pitched low and I wasn't sure if he actually meant for me to hear it.

"C'mon," I said, and headed up for the door.

×

I look more like my mother than I do my father. Both of them look fairly average, but I have my mother's eyes and her caramelly brown hair and all that. I have my father's bad eyesight.

It was my mother who answered the door. "Ashton!" she said. "Guillaume."

"Hello, Mrs. Collins," Guillaume said. He sounded bored. He sounded like he always had when he'd come over to my house when we'd been little: like he was dying for the adults to go away so he could do what he really wanted to do. For Guillaume (at least at that point in his life) that was goad me into helping him torture and kill small animals or read. Probably it hadn't changed much. "Your house hasn't changed a bit."

My mother laughed, a little, but I could tell she wasn't having a good time. "We're too busy to redecorate, I guess," she said. "Come in, both of you."

We went in.

It was weird, but I truly hadn't been home for more than an evening since before I'd gone to college. Guillaume had been taking up all of my time. Everything was the same. Both of my parents were lawyers, and busy ones at that, and they didn't have the time to decorate for Easter— or Christmas, or Halloween, et cetera. I had a lot of treeless Christmases as a child. It had never really bothered me all that much.

Guillaume's parents hired people to decorate for them for most major holidays. Everything except Halloween. Back before the island, instead of hiring someone to decorate for Halloween, they just gave Guillaume a credit card and let him loose in Spirit Halloween. It was maybe the most understanding they'd ever shown of their son. As a result, their house looked like... well, a Spirit Halloween all October.

As we walked in, I asked Guillaume, "Do your parents still have all those animatronics you used to buy for Halloween?"

Guillaume glanced at me. "Yes. In storage. Why?"

"Just thinking," I said. "It would be fun to dig them out."

"Why?" Guillaume said. "We can just buy new ones?"

I shrugged. I let myself drift, briefly, thinking about a future where we had a house, a big one, a scary one, with animatronics everywhere, even when it wasn't Halloween. It was like the kind of ideas I'd had as a kid. Stuff we'd talk about when we'd stay up late on the island staring at the fire or in the cave.

Always together. We were always together and talking about how life would be when we grew up.

Well, now we were grown up and we were killing people.

"Are the cousins coming?" I asked Mom as she followed us in.

"No," she said. "It'll just be us. And Guillaume, of course."

"Okay," I said. As she disappeared into the kitchen, I elbowed Guillaume softly in the side. "You scared off all my cousins."

"Good," Guillaume said. "You never liked them, anyway."

. chapter twenty-three .

"So what are you majoring in, Guillaume?"

"English literature."

"You think grad school's in your future?"

"Probably."

"Maybe you can give some of that motivation to Ashton." This was of course, my father, who had been interrogating Guillaume like he was my lover—which, well, he sort of was, but we weren't about to tell my family that—before prom night. "We're trying to convince him that law school would be a good idea."

"Sure," Guillaume said. "Then he can get me off next time."

I choked on my scalloped potatoes.

"That was a joke," Guillaume said. He smiled angelically. "I'm cured."

"I'm sure you are," my mother said. Guillaume hadn't eaten much—of real food, that was. I had seen him surreptitiously shove a couple handfuls of jellybeans into his pockets, so I figured he was chewing on those instead of the ham and scalloped potatoes.

"They wouldn't have let me out otherwise," Guillaume said. "I have coping mechanisms now. Did you know that people who watch horror movies and listen to heavy metal music are actually less violent than others? They can get all their rage out with the fictional things and don't have to hurt real people anymore. I started writing."

I stared at him. I either didn't know about this or he was making it up. He wouldn't meet my eyes.

"I'm writing a zombie book right now," he said. "Lots of blood and guts."

"Oh," my mother said. I kicked Guillaume under the table, but he still didn't look at me. He was still smiling angelically at my parents. Like he was saying things that were normal—and maybe they would have been, if they hadn't been coming from him. If they hadn't been coming from a serial killer in the making.

"What are some of the books you've been reading this semester?" my father asked. He was trying to save it.

Good fucking luck, Dad.

"For school?" Guillaume said. When my father nodded, he started listing. "*Frankenstein, Titus Andronicus*—oh, and for Young Adult Literature, *Lord of the Flies*. My paper for that one's going to be good. I can tell. I didn't have to read it for high school, and I really enjoy how Golding managed to get a real horror novel onto ninth grade reading curricula."

I hadn't had to read *Lord of the Flies,* either, mostly because the teacher had taken a look at my history, patted me on the head, and given me *Night* by Elie Wiesel instead. I hadn't complained, because *Night* was about half the size of *Lord of the Flies*, but I really wondered why she thought it was any less stimulating in the gore department. Wiesel doesn't hold back on his descriptions of the horrors of the Holocaust or anything.

"I guess I should say I wasn't allowed to read it in high school," Guillaume said. "The doctors thought it would be bad for me. But reading it now, since I'm cured and all, I can appreciate it as literature, and not get sucked back into some kind of post-traumatic flashback or something."

"Right," my father said.

My mother was looking decidedly green. Guillaume really was turning on the charm.

"Personally, I'm reading *Book of the Dead*," Guillaume said. "It's for research for my own book. It's a book of short stories by various horror authors about zombies. My favorite one so far has been the one that's clearly just a zombie parody of Bret Easton Ellis's *Less than Zero*, and—"

My mother dropped her fork and very quickly left the room. Guillaume shut his mouth.

Smiled again.

"I'm sorry, Guillaume," my father said. "She's had a hard time adjusting to the idea that you were back in Ashton's life."

"Don't worry about it," Guillaume said. Then, finally, he met my eyes. There was nothing behind them. They were back to the dead-fish stare, the stare that he used whenever he was talking to someone besides me—unless, of course, he was hurting them. He smiled. He looked like a shark. "I don't mind. I'm cured."

. chapter twenty-four .

We were going to have to wait to kill Nicky until summer vacation.

"We'll road trip," Guillaume said. "Just us. We'll get Nicky and then we'll go for Adam."

"Why not Kevin?" I asked.

Guillaume grimaced. "He has more security," he said. "Adam's living a fairly normal life. He'll be easier to get."

The unfortunate part that we both knew was that, after Adam, we were done. Adam was a big name. He'd done interviews with popular true crime podcasts, he'd done documentaries, and he was the *hero*. Kevin was the villain in the same way; no matter which one we had decided to go after, it would have been our last one.

"We've got quite a bit of list before Adam and Kevin," I said.

"Quality over quantity, Ash," Guillaume said, giving me a sardonic look. We were studying for finals, then; or rather, *I* was. Guillaume would pass all of his without much work. His brain worked well for academia. "Besides, if we keep killing the cannon fodder, they'll realize, anyway. Eventually. I'd like to get at least one of the big guns before the end."

"I guess," I said. I was more of a quantity over quality guy. "So where are Nicky and Adam?"

Guillaume grinned. "Michigan," he said. "Both of them."

×

Guillaume hired movers and all that for the shit we had in the dorm, and I texted my mom to let her know that we were going on a road trip this summer. She didn't even call me back, which really made me think that she'd given up on her only son, but it was fine. It made it easier for us to do what we needed to do. "They'll drop off our stuff in a storage unit in town," Guillaume said, crunching on one of those giant lollipops that they mostly sell to six-year-olds. Guillaume eating lollipops was always interesting, mostly because he didn't lick them. He just bit. "So next year, if by some miracle, we're not rotting in prison by then, we can just have them set it up again."

"Are they who set up your stuff this year?"

"Yes," Guillaume said.

×

The idea of us counting down to it, to some massive end to our journey, our year of killing; *that* was one part terrifying, one part exciting. Part of me still figured that when we got caught, Guillaume would take most of the blame again. Because of course he would.

I've always been just a follower. Easy to influence.

If there's someone to blame, it's Guillaume Argot.

. chapter twenty-five .

It was about a fourteen-hour drive from our small private liberal arts college to Nicky Wilder's family farm in Michigan, but we took our time. I drove most of the way. We stopped in seedy motels, not because we couldn't afford the good ones but because, I think, they fit the ambience. We fucked in the seedy motels, too. Everything was starting to move faster.

"Wilder's a warm-up," Guillaume said as my SUV passed the *WELCOME TO MICHIGAN* sign on the side of the highway. "We'll get rid of him quick, and then we'll be really fun with Adam."

"Why not just skip him, then?" I said. "If he's just a warm-up."

"I want body parts," Guillaume said. "To scatter, you know."

"Oh, right," I said. "Naturally. Like anyone normal. Do we need to stop at Wal-Mart for totes? You know, for your body parts of Nicky Wilder that you want to scatter around like, just for the vibes?"

Guillaume glared at me, but then he grinned, a little, and laughed, and looked out the window, and I was so in love with him I thought my heart would burst. I would have done anything for him at that moment. I would have given him my own insides, if he needed them. Just slit open my belly and handed them over. "That's actually a good idea," he said. "Save me from having to pay to have your car reupholstered."

"Wh—you were just going to *throw them in the back of my car?*"

×

We got a hotel room at the closest town to Nicky Wilder's family farm. "Farm boys do chores," Guillaume said. "We'll stay up and head out there at two or three. He'll be up to do chores."

"Are you sure?" I asked.

Guillaume glared at me.

"Sure, fine," I said. "He'll be up to do chores. What do they have? Animals?"

"Pigs," Guillaume said, and I choked.

"Seriously?" I said. "They have *pigs*?"

"They have pigs," Guillaume said. "I looked into it. Pigs are great, because anything we don't need, we can just feed to the pigs."

"Pigs," I muttered. I hadn't touched or seen a pig in real life, outside of like, a petting zoo, since high school. We'd dissected fetal pigs. Me and my partner had gotten a good grade, mostly because I was willing to really get my hands in there where some of the others weren't. "So, what. We catch him, we cut him up, we throw what we want in the tote and what we don't in with the pigs?"

"That's about it," Guillaume said. I was lying on our bed in the hotel room and he was standing on it. Jumping on it, really. I kept waiting for him to, either on accident or on purpose, jump on me and break a rib or something. He kicked at my side lightly. "I'll distract him and you get behind him and cut off his air until he passes out. I'll cut his throat and then we can do what we need to do."

"I can cut his throat," I said.

Guillaume stopped jumping for a second and then sat down on my stomach, his feet coming up to pin my arms down. I stayed limp. He didn't weigh enough to make me have trouble breathing or anything. He was just pressure. "That's right," he said. "You can kill. I forgot."

"I don't know how," I said. He dug the toe of his left foot into the crook of my elbow and I winced. "Remember, Gill, I am perfect for you. I kill people and I let you beat me up whenever you want."

"Right," Guillaume said. I put up my knees and he leaned against them. I made a good chair for him. He looked like he was comfortable. "If you don't get him right away… he could be a tough one. He's big now, remember."

"Look him up again," I said.

He rolled off of me and grabbed his phone, and then pulled my hair until I sat up next to him. He opened up Instagram and showed me Nicky Wilder's profile. "Holy shit," I muttered. "Prom king? I wasn't prom king."

"Neither was I," Guillaume said, and I guess that was meant to be a joke, because of the whole psych ward and everything, but I settled for glaring at him. He ignored me. "But look at him. He's big. How tall are you?"

"I dunno," I said. "Five ten, maybe."

"Wilder's at least six even," Guillaume said. "How much do you weigh?"

"One forty?" I guessed. "I'm not as scrawny as you, but—"

"I think you're scrawnier," Guillaume said. "I think I'm more compact. You're skinny like a Nerds Rope."

"Whatever," I said. "I'm tall enough to cut his throat, all right? Unless you desperately want to be the one to do the deed."

. chapter twenty-six .

Nicky Wilder was a bit player, so Guillaume didn't actually care who did the deed as long as he ended up dead, and that was why I was standing, hiding, up to my ankles in pig shit, waiting for him to come out to the barn. Guillaume was still willing to be the decoy. We were hoping that Wilder would be so weirded out—and Guillaume could be creepy as fuck, even when he didn't try, so I was a little excited to see how creepy he'd be if he really turned on the Hannibal Lector charm—that I could sneak up behind him and cut his throat without too much of a fuss.

  Guillaume was hiding, too, on the other side of the barn. It was four thirty in the morning. Wilder should be coming out soon. When he did, Guillaume would start making noise, and if he had to, he'd talk. Guillaume could spew all sorts of bullshit when it came down to it. Probably it was the English major thing.

  Also, I figure the fact that he read about five hundred books a year helped. You can't consume that many words and not have them stick in your head.

  I crossed my arms and tried not to breathe so deep. I shifted, a little, while I could; once Wilder got to the barn, I couldn't move. Not until he was sufficiently distracted. A few of the pigs came over and sniffed at me, but since I was upright and could conceivably fight back, they weren't trying to take a bite out of me. They mostly seemed mildly curious. I figure that would be different when we started throwing bloody bits of flesh in with them. Then that mild curiosity would probably turn into serious curiosity.

And hunger.

The door at the front of the barn cracked open and a large shape filled the space. My heart dropped into my stomach. Wilder really *had* gotten big; he was broad, he'd filled out, he could snap either me or Guillaume over his knee without really trying. He wasn't like Ryan Spencer, who'd run fat.

Fuck.

I heard a crash on the other side of the barn—Guillaume, I figured—and Wilder glanced over that way. "Cain?" he called. "That you, pup?"

"No," Guillaume said, and his voice floated out of the darkness in a way that made me shiver. And made me hard, to be honest. The thought of Guillaume lurking in a dark corner of a barn like some sort of fucking creepypasta made me hard.

"Who's there?" Wilder asked. He sounded older, gruffer than he should have, and when he fumbled for the light, when he got it on, I realized our mistake.

This wasn't Nicky Wilder.

It was his father.

If Guillaume was shocked about it, he didn't let on; he kept going. Which I figured meant I should keep going, too. Guillaume stepped into the light and I crouched down, a little. Wilder Senior wasn't looking at me; Guillaume had done his job as distraction well enough, but I crouched anyway. A pig came over and started snuffling at my hand, and I smacked its snout lightly. Insistent, it started tugging at the bottom of my T-shirt.

I smacked it again.

"Who're you?" Wilder Senior said.

"Guillaume Argot," Guillaume said. "I don't know if we met. We were definitely at the courthouse at the same time. Nicky testified against me."

Wilder Senior seemed to realize that he was in a precarious position here, but I figure that he figured he could take the skinny son-of-a-bitch that was Guillaume Argot. And even better, Guillaume was legally an adult now, so he could knock him flat and not get it for beating up on a minor.

"What are you doing here?" Wilder Senior asked.

"Well, I was waiting for Nicky," Guillaume said. "You giving him the morning off? I know he's home from school. I follow him on Instagram."

"That's none of your business," Wilder Senior said, and I figured this was as good of an opening as I was going to get, so I crawled through the boards of the pig pen, my T-shirt tearing—I let it go, the pig would swallow it or something—and standing. Wilder Senior must have seen movement at the corner of his eye or something, because he turned to look at me, but I ducked behind a post.

I closed my eyes and waited. "What are you looking at?" Guillaume asked.

"Must be one of the pigs," Wilder Senior said. "I know none of those boys would be helping you."

"Right," Guillaume said. "They all testified against me. I wouldn't even want their help."

I figured Wilder Senior wasn't looking anymore, so I peeked. His back was to me. I reached into my pocket and pulled out Guillaume's blade and flicked it open. It felt right, in my hand. I was going to have to jump, a little, and get my arms around Wilder Senior so that I could really jab the knife into his throat, but he wasn't *that* much taller than me. I just wanted to jump so I could get some leverage.

I crept closer.

"So, what's your plan?" Wilder Senior asked. He looked relaxed; he was just, as far as he knew, facing Guillaume, who did look pretty harmless when he wasn't covered in blood and grinning his shark grin. He probably still saw Guillaume as the same twelve-year-old who got locked up like a crazy person. He figured he could take that twelve-year-old.

He didn't know about me.

I jumped, and landed on his back, and started stabbing. Wilder Senior made a noise, some kind of dying animal noise, and slammed me into a post. My head hit it and I saw stars, but by the time I was collapsed on the ground, he was bleeding. Bleeding good. He was breathing hard and bleeding on me—his back to Guillaume, which was the worst decision he could probably make—and he knelt on my stomach and grabbed me by the hair and lifted my head. It hurt. I gritted my teeth. I couldn't smell anything but blood.

"Collins kid," he managed. "Figured. You were always a creep, too."

Those were his last words. Guillaume cut his throat so wide his head nearly came off and I was bathed in blood. The hand convulsed in my hair and then the body was on me, crushing me. "*Gill, c'mon,*" I said through gritted teeth.

"One second," Guillaume said, and yanked. Nicky Wilder's dad was big. Heavy. "This'll work fine. I just needed the insides, anyway. We can pretend they came from Nicky."

"Sure," I gasped. I wiped at my face. Not that it helped clear it up any; my hands were as covered in blood as my face was at this point. "I need a breather."

"Stay out of the pig pens," Guillaume said. "They'd probably take a bite out of you smelling like that."

I flipped him off and watched him butcher Wilder Senior. He layered the man's clothes in the tote and he did it all with such a *medical* efficiency.

Guillaume took the intestines, the stomach, the kidneys, and the liver. He took the heart. He hammered at the skull for a while but he didn't have the strength to crack it so he left the brain alone. He took the lungs, but only put one of them in the tote. He cut the other one open to look at it.

"Wow," he muttered. He traced his hands over the flesh like it was soft fabric. "This feels *weird*. Ash, come feel this."

"I'm good," I croaked. "Still trying to breathe."

Guillaume gave me a pointed look and cut off a piece. A small piece. Bite-sized.

"Are we doing that again?" I said. "I really can't keep up, Gill. I did it on the island 'cause I was hungry, but—"

Guillaume gave me another look and crawled over to me and offered it. Put it right up to my mouth.

"You first," I said.

He bit off half of it, chewed, swallowed, and offered it again. I ate from his hands and licked his fingers clean. He was smiling. He was smiling. He was smiling some kind of combination between the scary smile and the smile only I got; the real smile, the turned-on smile, the smile that told me I'd pleased him. He touched me, then, with his hand, sliding down to touch my skin where the pig had torn my shirt. His other hand, the one still sticky with blood, on my jaw, and he kissed me.

I kissed him back.

. chapter twenty-seven .

I don't think I have to tell you that when we got back to the hotel room, once we'd run a cold bath and Guillaume threw on a coat to cover his blood-stained clothes and got some ice and we stuck the tote with organs into the water, so they'd be at least relatively fresh, we fucked again. Still covered in blood, sticky, smelling like iron and pigshit.

. chapter twenty-eight .

"How can I explain this to someone who played *sports*," Guillaume said, dragging out the word like it was the worst thing he could think of. "*This* is our SuperBowl. Our World Series. Our—what is it for hockey?"

"Stanley Cup," I said.

"After this, it's over," Guillaume said. "So we better do a fucking good job."

I nodded. We'd refreshed the ice in the bath a few times and the organs didn't look too bad. I wouldn't trust them to be transplanted into anyone's body or anything, but for the purposes of scattering them around and freaking out Adam Nicholson, they'd do fine.

"I can't believe we're still walking free, honestly," I said. "We made a mess at the Wilder house."

"Pigs ate most of it," Guillaume said. He grinned at me, his shark grin. The you're-fucked grin. "Besides, nobody knows we're in Michigan now. The last couple of times people knew we were around."

"I guess," I said. I was still sore from how Wilder Senior had thrown me around the night before, and I said as much to Guillaume.

"Well," Guillaume said. "Adam'll probably be easier to subdue."

×

Adam Nicholson was and always had been the quintessential golden boy. He was tall, attractive, broad-shouldered, and blond. Of course, now one of his hands was gone at the wrist, but I'd seen interviews and he dealt with that like he dealt with everything else: with enough humility and grace to make any housewife watching from home soaking wet. In school, he'd been on the track team and he'd been involved in student government. He'd been popular but nice to the losers. He'd even tried to befriend Guillaume a few times.

It hadn't worked, but he'd tried.

Now, he lived in a cabin a few miles back from his parents' house. It was still on his parents' property, but it gave him some sort of privacy. Guillaume, through the power of having more money than God, had found out that Adam did school online.

He rarely left the cabin.

"So our boy's gone agoraphobic," I said as I coasted down the highway. The organs were sealed up tight in the tote but I was not looking forward to when they started to smell, because I was *sure* they were going to.

"That is what it looks like," Guillaume said. He was chewing on his thumbnail and studying Google Maps. Adam didn't live too far from the Wilders, but it was far enough to make me a little jumpy about having a plastic tote full of organs in my trunk. We'd thrown a blanket over it and everything, but still.

I turned up the music.

"Turn left," Guillaume said.

I turned left.

×

All the lights were on in the cabin. We'd parked the car on the side of the road, at an approach, a mile or so back, and trekked through the woods. I felt like some kind of bumbling idiot, but Guillaume was quiet as a cat. He really was good at this sort of thing. This stalking, hunting, killing thing.

Of course I knew that already. It was *Guillaume*.

But that didn't mean it wasn't beautiful to watch in action.

"Motherfucker's scared," Guillaume said, his voice pitched low.

"Of course he is," I said. I counted off on my fingers. "Ryan Spencer, Richard Ayers, Vic Walsh, and now Nicky Wilder's dad. Maybe he doesn't know about the last one yet, but he will, and he definitely knows about the first three. He's put it together. If Vic put it together, Adam put it together."

"Or maybe he just always sleeps with the lights on," Guillaume said.

"Maybe he's not asleep," I said. "Maybe he's up waiting for us."

"I hope he is," Guillaume said. "More fun then."

Then, quick as a ghost, he slipped past me and toward the cabin. He was a shadow on the grass, flitting in and out of spots of light like a moth; reverse Mothman, I thought, and then I followed. I wasn't near as graceful, but I was graceful enough.

"I'll take the upstairs," Guillaume said. "You take downstairs."

I nodded. Guillaume then pulled off his backpack, in which he'd shoved the organs, and started scattering them over the back porch. I held my sleeve over my nose. They fucking stank.

"All the trouble to get them," I muttered. "And you're just putting them on the back porch."

"Some are for the front door," Guillaume said. "You go in. I'll deal with this."

I tried the door. It was locked.

"Oh, Jesus," Guillaume muttered, and then punched out the window on the door for me, then reached in and unlocked it. His hand was streaked red with blood. He didn't care anymore. They'd find blood here, and fingerprints, and everything, and it would point to Guillaume and he didn't care because this was our Bonnie and Clyde moment.

"Thanks," I muttered, and then I headed inside.

It felt strange, and wrong, to do this without Guillaume. My heart constricted, a little, and I thought for a second that, *maybe*, Guillaume was pulling one over on me. That he was going to call the cops or something and I'd take the fall for everything and—

But that was stupid. His blood was everywhere and he'd been with me every other time.

The cabin was one of those ones that looked rustic on the outside but was doped out on the inside; marble countertops, flat-screen TVs, all that stuff. Adam had spent his island money, and he'd spent it well. Adam had gotten more than any of us, really—he'd been the hero. Most of us had been cast as bit players who got bit player money, no matter what had really gone down.

There was nobody in the kitchen, which was where the door at the back porch led to. There was an empty bowl, a big one, in the sink, and I reached down and felt the inside. My fingers came away greasy and I sucked them clean. Butter.

Popcorn.

"A-*dam*," I whispered. "Am I interrupting date night?"

No response, but then again, I hadn't really expected one. Probably, Adam was tucked away nice in bed. I was just downstairs to double-check. Guillaume would get to do the real killing.

The TV was off. I grabbed the remote and turned it back on.

He'd been watching *Brooklyn-99*. Lame.

I hit play and jacked up the volume.

I heard footsteps.

I figured it was probably Gill, so I didn't turn around. Then I felt an arm around my neck, an arm that ended in a hand, a *real* hand, and then another hand over my mouth, and both of them were much too big to be Guillaume's, and then my face made contact with that nice marble countertop and I fell to the ground, gasping for air. I scrambled away, backwards, pushing myself back with my feet, and I looked up.

I recognized this guy.

"Fucking *you*?" I said.

The name escaped me. The name fucking escaped me. The guy had been on the island, I *knew* he had, but he was—he'd been bit player of bit player, this one, he'd been on the football team but he hadn't been too important, and he'd been—

"Ashton Collins," the bit player said. "You always were a fucking creep."

Then he stabbed me in the stomach and, honestly, ripped my fucking guts out.

PEOPLE TO KILL BY GUILLAUME ARGOT

1. ~~Ashton Collins~~
2. Kevin Thomson
3. Adam Nicholson
4. Ryan Spencer :)
5. Erik Marsh
6. Zach Blanchard
7. Jeff Frederick
8. Richard Ayers :)
9. Seth Hinton
10. Nicky Wilder
11. Vic Walsh :) :)
12. Stephen Murphy
13. Johnny Hopkins
14. Leo Moore
15. William Black

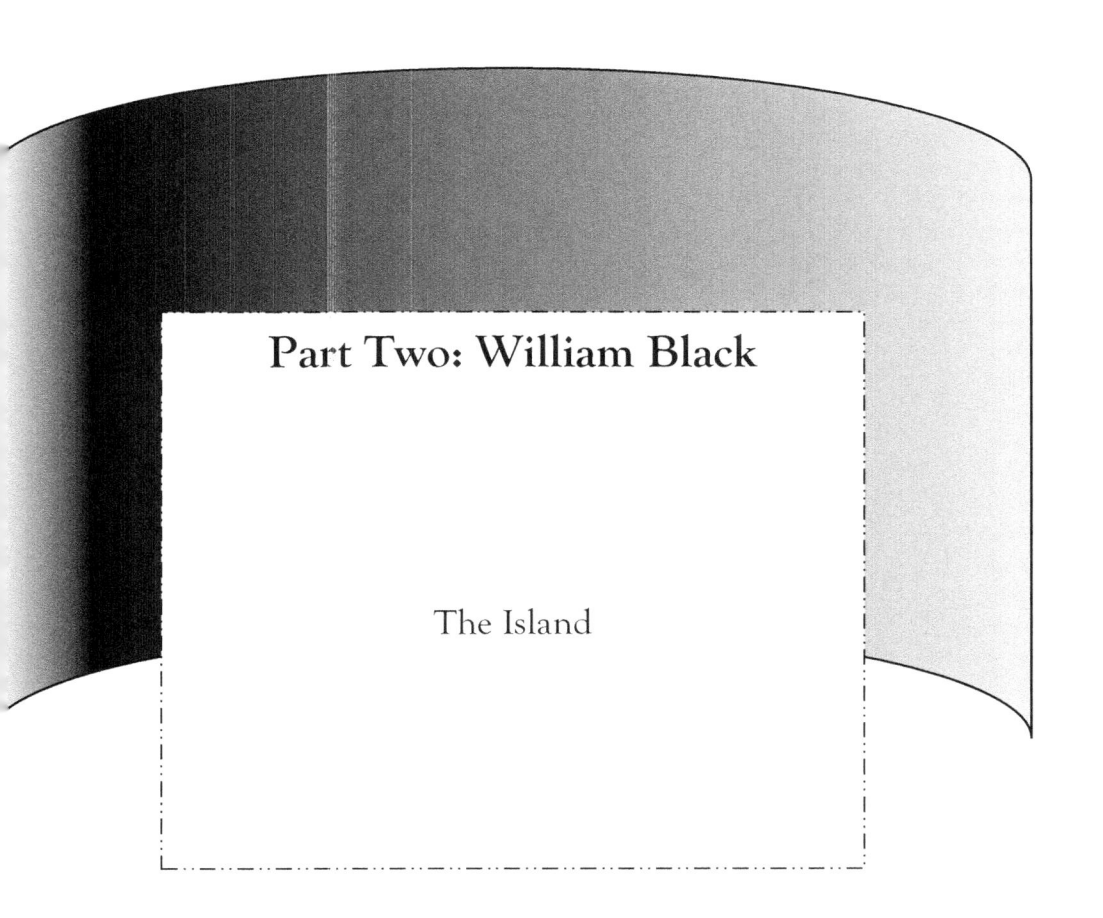

Part Two: William Black

The Island

LIST OF SURVIVORS OF PLANE CRASH ON BOLIN ISLAND

1. Argot, Guillaume
2. Ayers, Richard
3. Barron, Terrell
4. Bates, Jaxson
5. Berry, Connor
6. Black, William
7. Blanchard, Zach
8. Byers, Billy
9. Cantrell, Alfonso
10. Collins, Ashton
11. Cooke, Luca
12. Dale, Laurence
13. Foley, Efrain
14. Frederick, Jeff
15. Green, Cody
16. Hinton, Seth
17. Hopkins, Johnny
18. Horton, Sage
19. Howard, James
20. Hudson, Tommy
21. Hurley, Sawyer
22. Johnson, Lucas
23. Larson, Elian
24. Marsh, Erik
25. Martin, Liam
26. May, Jayden
27. McCrag, Cullen
28. Moore, Leo
29. Murphy, Steven
30. Murray, Tyler
31. Nicholson, Adam
32. Ortega, Jonathan

33. Reid, Callum
34. Riley, Cameron
35. Rogers, Reuben
36. Rogers, Briggs
37. Simmons, Charlie
38. Smith, Caleb
39. Spencer, Ryan
40. Thomson, Kevin
41. Walsh, Victor
42. Wilder, Nicholas

. chapter one .

Will woke up and it was hot. There were bugs, too; he could hear them, all around him, a constant racket that was making his head hurt worse. His head hurt, and *he* hurt, like he'd been hit by a truck or something.

 He sat up and breathed in deep. His ribs stung, but they didn't stab. He hoped that meant he didn't have any broken ribs or anything. He'd never had a broken rib but last month when Sage Horton had gone tumbling down the stairs at school he'd come back from the hospital with a note getting him out of Phys Ed and tape on his chest. The school believed it had been from that tumble since Sage's dad was already in jail.

 He didn't see anyone around.

 He didn't know where he was.

 He pushed himself to his feet. He wavered, a little, but he rubbed at his eyes and shook his head (which did not help the headache; it sent his brain sloshing around like it was on rough waters), and focused.

 Focus, Will, focus.

 As he focused, it started to come back. The plane, the fire, scrambling to get a parachute on and holding his breath and jumping. He didn't remember landing but he guessed he must have done all right if he was still alive.

 He was still tangled up in his parachute, and he wriggled out of it, leaving it on the forest floor. He stepped out of it and looked around. It was hot. It was that sticky kind of hot, the humid kind of hot, and it was making his shirt stick to his neck.

He loosened his tie. They'd been on the plane in their uniforms, which meant a tie, pinchy shoes, slacks, button-ups, and jackets. Will had taken off the jacket because it had been hard to get comfortable in and now it was gone. Gone with the plane.

Fuck it. If they'd landed on… whatever they'd landed on, he didn't need to wear a tie. He finished taking it off and chucked it into the brush.

"Will," he heard, and glanced around. "Will, up here."

He looked up.

Sage was hanging from a tree. His parachute had gotten tangled in it, somehow, and now he was stuck.

"Can you help?" Sage asked.

"Yeah, I can try," Will said. He crossed to stand by him. He could reach Sage's knees, pretty much, from where he was. "Do you know where we are?"

"I'm in a fucking tree," Sage said, and Will snorted. A lot of people didn't get close enough to Sage to get snark from him, but the kid could cuss like a sailor and make fun of people out of the corner of his mouth with the best of them. Will liked him. And a lot people thought Sage was a scaredy-cat, mostly because he was so jumpy all the time, but he'd testified against his dad. That had to take some balls. "Can you climb and get me down, maybe?"

"I can try," Will said again. He got closer to the trunk of the tree. He might be able to pull himself up. There was a branch, the one that Sage had gotten caught on, low enough that if he jumped, he could catch it, and then sort of just… walk his way up the trunk, maybe? He wished someone like Richard Ayers was around. Ayers was always in trees and shit. Will could climb a tree, sure, but…

Focus, Will, focus.

He jumped and caught the branch with both hands. It bent, a little, jogging Sage up and down, and Sage yelped. Will's feet scrabbled uselessly at the trunk before he fell. "*Shit*," Will said.

"Try again," Sage said.

Will jumped again, with the same result.

"Don't *leave me up here*."

This time, when Will tried, he didn't get anywhere... but his weight was enough to, finally, make the limb come crashing down, bringing Sage with it. Will crawled over to him and tried to fumble him free of the parachute. Sage's face was white; whether with exertion or pain, Will didn't know. "Ow," he muttered, and pushed himself up to sit.

"Are you okay?" Will asked.

Sage gave him a look. "As okay as I can be, I guess," he said. He shivered, a little, and then took off his own tie. His elbows and knees had been shredded, probably from his fall through the trees. Will must have missed them. He didn't remember jack shit about his landing. "I wonder if anyone else lived."

"There were eighty kids and twenty adults on that plane," Sage said. "We're not the only ones. I just hope it's normal people that lived."

"Like who? Adam?" Will said.

"Adam'd be okay," Sage said.

And like a dog-whistle, almost, as a sign that shit was not okay, that normal people didn't live, Ashton Collins appeared at the edge of their little clearing, breathing hard, covered in blood. "Guys? Guys, come help. Gill's hurt."

. chapter two .

Ashton Collins and Guillaume Argot weren't exactly bullies, but they were creeps. Will was pretty sure they tortured small animals together in their free time. Sage was pretty sure Guillaume had pushed him down the stairs a few weeks before the plane crash. If you got Ashton away from Guillaume, he could be sort-of normal. More like it was he Xerox'd the personality of whoever he was with and copied it over his Guillaume-personality.

  Ashton was the only person Guillaume let call him "Gill." He was tall, stringbean tall, and had hair that mostly ran to greasy, and walked all slouched over like he didn't know what to do with his height.

  Right about now he was talking about a mile a minute.

  "It's *bad*, the cut's *bad*, he's really hurt, we gotta sew it up or something, I don't know what to do, he's gonna *die*—"

  "Is that so bad?" Sage muttered, out of the corner of his mouth, and Will elbowed him.

  "He cut himself when we were landing, we landed pretty close but he landed on a rock or something and his knee is just—it's just cut *open*, I can see his *kneecap*—" Ashton was still going.

  Eventually, they came to another small clearing. Guillaume was in the center of it, staring dispassionately up at the sky. His one pant leg had been cut off above the knee.

  Will could see a lot of blood.

  A lot.

"Gill, I found Will and Sage," Ashton said, hurrying back over to him. Guillaume propped himself up on his elbows and looked at them. Will felt a shiver go up his spine. Looking into Guillaume's eyes was like staring into the eyes of a shark. They were so cold and black and impersonal.

"What the fuck are they going to do?" Guillaume said. His voice was tight. He was pale—paler than usual.

"I don't *know*, but I don't know what to do!" Ashton said. "Besides, Horton's always patching himself up."

Will looked at Sage, who rolled his eyes.

"Sure," Guillaume said. He flopped back onto the ground. Ashton was kneeling by his head. "Do your worst."

Will drew closer, and when he saw the state of Guillaume's knee, *really* saw it, up close, he almost upchucked. Ashton was right. You could see the kneecap. The flesh had been cut so neatly that it was like someone had just taken a butcher knife to it.

"Oh, jeez," he muttered.

"That's the understatement of the century," Guillaume said. Will was pretty sure he'd never heard Guillaume talk this much in his *life*; maybe he was chatty around Ashton, since the two of them only seemed to be able to part when Ashton had football practice, but around everyone else he was, normally, dead silent. He wouldn't answer questions in class and if you were unlucky enough to be his partner for a project he would do exactly half and then ignore you. But maybe getting his knee cut open was loosening his lips a little.

"This definitely needs stitches," Sage said. He'd edged closer.

"You see it enough on yourself to know that, Horton?" Guillaume snapped.

"Yeah," Sage said. He chewed on his lower lip. Will could practically see the gears moving in his head. "We need a needle and thread. I mean, we could use the cord from the parachute, but a needle…"

"Gill has a knife," Ashton said. "We could use it to poke holes in his skin and then—"

"Like *fuck you are doing that*," Guillaume said.

"Shut *up*, Gill, do you want to bleed to death?"

Guillaume put his arms over his death. "I will kill anyone who pokes holes in my skin so that they can thread parachute wire through the holes to stitch my knee together. I am not joking, or hyperbolizing. That is what I will do. Slowly. With the knife."

"Gill, nobody knows what hyperbolizing means," Ashton said. He looked around at them, anxious. "Do you s'pose maybe if we just tied it up real tight…"

"It'd be better than letting him bleed all over the ground," Sage said. "But that really needs stitches. Can I see that knife?"

Ashton came up with the knife. It was a pocketknife, but it looked too big and scary to be anywhere legal for a twelve-year-old to be carrying it. Sage went over to what Will supposed was Guillaume's parachute, if the blood was any indication, and used the knife to tear off a piece that seemed relatively dry.

"I'll use the string to tie it tight," he said. "Hopefully tight enough that it'll stop bleeding and sort of sew together on its own."

Guillaume was silent.

Ashton kept bouncing around, nervous. "Will he be okay?"

"I don't know," Sage said. "I'm not a doctor. I'm thirteen."

"Will he die?" Ashton asked. "I don't want him to die, please don't let him die, we'll be good if he doesn't die."

"I'm not Jesus," Sage said. "I can't heal him or anything. I can just tie this up real tight. Not so tight that he loses the leg or anything."

"If my leg falls off, I will kill you," Guillaume muttered.

Sage wrapped the parachute material—Will didn't know exactly what it was, but it was plasticky, almost— tight around Guillaume's leg, and then tied it off with the cord. "You have to keep it clean," he told Ashton. "We have to find… water, or something, to clean it out with. And you have to keep it clean."

"I'll keep it clean," Ashton said. "I promise."

Sage opened his mouth to say more when they heard it. It took them all a couple of minutes to realize what it was before Ashton let out a quick bark of laughter. "Jeez, did Nicholson find his *trumpet*?"

"Is he calling us all together?" Sage said, glancing around at them under long, dark bangs. "I mean, if it's him, and not…" He trailed off.

"Not who?" Ashton said. "Someone who found the trumpet? Some kind of adult?"

"Yeah," Sage said. He grimaced. "I hope some kind of adult survived the fall. But they ushered us all off first, didn't they? I mean, did you see any adults jumping?"

Will shook his head and, after a minute or two, Ashton shook his head, too. The trumpet kept blaring in the background. Guillaume's eyes were closed but Will was pretty sure he was still conscious; he kept clenching and unclenching his fist.

"Are you—" Ashton's voice was high, and reedy; it was almost to the level of panic it had been at when he'd stumbled upon them. "Are you saying that all of the adults—all the grown-ups—probably, they're all dead? Right? It's just us?"

Sage shrugged. "I *don't know*," he said. "I was hanging in a tree like, half an hour ago. But I didn't see any of them jump. I only saw kids jump."

"We're alone?" Ashton said. "Us, and whoever else survived."

In hindsight, Will wondered if Ashton was so freaked because he knew what he would do. What he and Guillaume would do without any adult supervision. If it was just kids and they were allowed to do whatever the hell they wanted.

In hindsight, Will wondered if maybe it would've been better if Ashton hadn't found Will and Sage, and Guillaume had just bled out on the forest floor.

. chapter three .

It was Adam Nicholson blowing on his trumpet, and there were about thirty other kids milling around. Some of them were kids that Will was surprised had survived the fall—Laurence Dale being one of them—but a lot of them were athletic kids.

A lot of them were football players, including Kevin. If Guillaume and Ashton weren't bullies but were generally creeps, Kevin was a bully. Him and Ryan Spencer kept most of the seventh grade in a general state of terror, for different reasons than Guillaume and Ashton did. They were the kids that would steal your lunch, push you down outside, and do all that sort of shit—Sage had gotten more than a couple bloody noses at Ryan Spencer's hands. Will, while he wasn't really as much of a target—he was forgettable, mostly, he figured; quiet, played football but wasn't too good or too bad at it, did OK in school but didn't raise his hand—had gotten snow shoved down the back of his shirt the year before around Christmas.

And yeah, of course both Ryan Spencer and Kevin Thomson had survived.

×

Will and Sage had collapsed under a tree, and just by virtue of traveling together, Ashton and Guillaume were right next to them. Ashton had carried Guillaume on his back, and he lowered him to the ground with more care than Will had thought he was capable of. Guillaume seemed barely-conscious, his eyelids fluttering and his face sticky with sweat, and Will couldn't help but watch as Ashton tried to adjust him to make him comfortable, brushing hair out of his face and making sure he had something to lean on, before sitting down next to him. Guillaume's head dropped to Ashton's shoulder.

Adam finished blowing on his trumpet when his face was spotty and red. He'd been going for fifteen minutes at least, and Will guessed Adam guessed that everyone else was dead—until they saw Richard Ayers, who was quiet but *nice*, drop down from a tree.

"Oh, jeez, Richie," Adam said, laughing a little. "Have you been there the whole time?"

Richard smiled at him in that sort of ditzy way he had, and then Adam cleared his throat and started.

"So," he said, projecting his voice like they'd been taught to when giving presentations in English class. "The plane crashed."

"No shit," Kevin called from the back.

Adam didn't get mad, just acknowledged him with a nod.

"We don't know where we are—I guess, I mean, *I* don't, and if you do, please tell me," Adam said, giving them a self-deprecating smile, and Will felt his heart swell, a little. If Adam could still make jokes, it couldn't be too bad. Adam Nicholson was a good guy. He was in student government, and ran track, and was so good at the trumpet that he'd been asked to bring it with so that, while they were on their class trip, he could perform at a ball game. That was why it had been on the plane and, despite a dent or two, it looked like it had survived the fall relatively well. Adam was tall and well-built and good-looking. He had light brown hair, almost blond, that curled softly around his ears and over his forehead, and he always had a smile for everyone, no matter if you were one of his friends, like Efrain Foley, who was something of a class clown, or the generally disliked Laurence Dale, who alternately complained and bragged, depending on how he was feeling when you caught him.

There was a rustle at the back of the group, where most of the football guys were, and Kevin stood up. Kevin was the antithesis of Adam—mean, didn't seem to like anyone, and even if he was good-looking, you wouldn't know by the scowl on his face. "Who put you in charge, Nicholson?" he said.

Adam shrugged. "Nobody, I guess," he said. "I just found my trumpet and figured it would be good to get together and talk—"

"About what?" Kevin said.

"He could tell you if you'd shut up, Thomson," Efrain Foley called, grinning a little. Efrain was tan because his family owned a beach house in Florida that they always went to on long weekends, no matter the season, and he had straight black hair that fell over his face and normally he spent his time making faces and cutting up in class. He was sharp, though.

Kevin flipped him off and Efrain pretended to die of a heart attack.

"All right, Ef, knock it off," Adam said, and Efrain, still flat on his back on the ground, gave him a salute. "Um. We have to figure out if this is an island or if it's connected to like, Florida or something."

"If it's connected to Florida we can all go to my house and *par-ty*," Efrain sang from the ground.

"Someone shut him up," Guillaume muttered, and when Will glanced over at him, his eyelids were half-open.

He was still sweating hard. Harder than the rest of them, and with the heat, they were all sweating pretty hard.

"Okay," Adam said. "Okay. Um, I think the first thing we should do, though, before that, is figure out who... survived."

It got quiet at that.

"Is anyone too badly hurt?"

Ashton shot to his feet. "Gill's hurt," he said. "He cut his knee open real bad. Um, Horton wrapped it up, but—" He cut himself off and shrugged helplessly. Guillaume, upon Ashton's standing, had ended up on the ground, his face pressed into the foliage. "—he's really bad. Like, he's really... he's hot."

Someone from the football team wolf-whistled.

"Like *warm*," Ashton said. "Like... like fevered."

Adam nodded a few times. "We'll have to try and find the first-aid kit," he said. "I know a lot of suitcases and stuff landed on the beach, just that way, where I found my trumpet. We've got to go through those. So, those are our three things we've got to do. A bunch of people should go through those. Hopefully the first-aid kit's there. Someone needs to write down everyone who's here. Before you run off doing whatever, give your name to..." He trailed off and glanced around.

"I'll do it," Sage said, raising his hand. "I can keep an eye on Guillaume, then, too."

"I'm not leaving Gill," Ashton said.

"You don't have to," Sage said. "I'm not gonna *carry* him, so I still need you for that."

Ashton nodded.

"Okay, awesome, thanks, Sage," Adam said. "I'll take a couple people to explore the island. Um..."

Amazingly, Will found himself raising his hand. Something about Adam's taking leadership like this made him want to participate. And anyway, Sage would be busy.

"Okay," Adam said. "So, Will... Efrain, yeah, you can come... okay, sure. Yeah. Kevin, Nicky. Everyone else should give your name to Sage and then go start looking through the suitcases, okay? We'll try to be back before too long. If it starts getting late we'll have to camp out, but..."

"I was a scout," Nicky yelled as he waded his way through the crowd. He was another football guy. Will got along with him fine. He wasn't nasty. He was a follower, sometimes, but he wasn't nasty, just kind of a dork. "I know how to make a fire."

"Awesome," Adam said. Will made his way to Adam. Efrain was already there, back on his feet, and Kevin joined them last, scowling around at them all. "So. We good to go?"

"Wouldn't be here if I wasn't," Kevin said sourly. He glanced around at them, apparently decided that Nicky was the least offensive to be around, and stood by him, and Will figured that he himself would walk alone in the middle of the party; Efrain would definitely be dogging Adam's steps the entire time. "So, what, are we just going to go to the beach and like, walk in a circle?"

"We could," Adam said. They started walking.

"That's going to take forever," Efrain said. "Also, if it's not an island, we'll just be walking and walking and walking and walking—"

"Shut up," Kevin said.

"He's got a point, though," Nicky said, and Kevin glared at him. "What? We should try and find the highest point. Have any of you guys seen like... a hill, or something?"

"So we're going to wander around until we find a hill?" Kevin said. "That could also take forever."

"What if we do both?" Will said. Everyone looked at him and he shrugged. "I mean, go to the beach, start walking, and if we see a hill, start going that way. Unless any of you guys have seen a hill."

"I saw a hill."

They all jumped.

Richard Ayers was there, a few feet away. Richard Ayers was small, and strange, but nice. Really liked animals.

"I was going to climb it but then I heard the trumpet," Richard said.

"Then you're coming with," Adam said. "All right."

Richard smiled at him and nodded, and took Efrain's spot next to Adam. Efrain pretended to faint and then realized that Will was the only one looking at him, so he twisted through the trees—which were, Will had to admit, pretty jungle-like—to join him. "And then there were six," Efrain intoned. He dropped his voice so the others couldn't hear them as Richard led the way through the trees. "Man, the way Kevin looked at us and then went for *Wilder* really hurt my self-esteem. Wilder's a dork. I woulda thought he'd go for you."

Will shrugged. "I spend too much time with Sage Horton," he said.

"I guess," Efrain said. He shook hair out of his face and reached up to slap a low-hanging branch. "And I don't play football, and Adam would spend all his time telling Kevin to stop bullying people. So I guess Wilder was the only choice."

"Besides, he's not that much of a dork," Will said. "He just…"

"*Oh, I was in scouts, I can start a fire,*" Efrain said, his voice high-pitched, even though his voice was naturally at a higher pitch than Nicky's. "*I was in scouts, so I can tell where north is without a compass. I was in scouts, so I can build a shelter for you, Kevin, just let me sleep at your feet like*—ow!"

Will glanced at him. Efrain was rubbing the back of his head. Kevin was looking far too innocent to actually be so, and Nicky was looking anywhere but the two of them.

"Motherfucker threw a rock at my head," Efrain muttered. He shuddered. "I hope it's not an island. I feel like it might get bad."

×

There was a hill—and they found it handily—but night fell faster than they knew what to do with. Nicky Wilder could, true to his word, build a fire, and so he did, and they crowded around it. The night made sounds around them that made them draw closer to each other; much to Efrain's distaste, Richard had glommed onto Adam so tightly, kept grabbing his arm, talking to him, that Efrain couldn't get a word in edgewise. Kevin was sullenly silent the entire time as Nicky stoked the fire, chattering brightly about scouts.

They didn't have anything to eat. That was hard. Will couldn't sleep. Nicky threw enough wood on the fire to keep it going through the night, and they all stretched out around it (Will wondered, briefly, what they would do if it rained, and then figured that he shouldn't think about it, just in case it ended up happening), and, one-by-one, everyone dropped off to sleep.

Everyone but Will.

He was just about there—the night was just too *spooky*; he could hear all sorts of bugs and animals and what if there was a bear?—when he heard the sound of someone crying. It was soft and muffled, like they were crying into their arm or something, and Will slowly pushed himself up to sit. The crying didn't stop, and Will glanced around at everyone. He'd expected it to be Richard, or Nicky, both of whom were sensitive in a way the others weren't, but he could see their faces clearly and they were asleep.

Efrain was curled up and shaking a few feet away.

Will crawled over to him and touched his shoulder. Efrain flinched.

"Ef, it's just me," Will said.

Efrain wiped at his face hurriedly and when he spoke his voice was strangled. "What do you want?"

"I just heard you," Will said. "What's…" He wanted to ask *wrong*, but he figured he knew what was wrong; they'd crashed on an island, some of them were hurt, all of them ached, and there was nobody telling them what to do or that it would be okay except for Adam Nicholson, and he was eleven. He wasn't even twelve yet. Most of them were twelve; it was May, and the school year was almost over, and they were almost eighth graders.

But Adam had a summer birthday.

"I want to go home," Efrain said, and his voice sounded small, and sad, and Will didn't know how Efrain would react if he gave him any sort of real comfort, so he stayed where he was, on his hands and knees, bending over him. "I want my mom."

He cried harder.

Will laid down next to him, back-to-back, and felt him shake with tears until they both fell asleep.

. chapter four .

It was definitely an island.

At the top of the hill that Richard had led them toward was a large clearing leading up to a waterfall, and they could see, very clearly, that they were on an island. It wasn't a very large island, but big enough, Will figured, that if they'd tried to circle it, it would have taken them a few days. They all stood, gaping. The clearing at the top of the hill was mostly rock, apart from the water. The waterfall was tall.

"Anyone wanna jump in?" Efrain said, giggling nervously. That morning, when Will had woken up, Efrain had already been at it, joking around and throwing random shit into the fire. They'd locked eyes once, and then Efrain had spent the rest of the day messing around with Richard. Not like, *mean* messing around—just messing with him, a little bit. Richard took it well enough. He generally took everything well enough.

Will walked to the edge of the waterfall and looked down. The water at the bottom looked deep, but…

It was a *high* fucking waterfall.

"There's our freshwater," Nicky said. "We should camp here."

"Ashton can wash out Guillaume's leg," Will said, mostly to himself, and he didn't realize that Adam was right next to him until he spoke.

"Guillaume looked rough at the meeting," Adam said.

"His knee's cut," Will said. "Down to the bone. Sage said he was gonna really look for a first aid kit in the suitcases. He wrapped it up good, but it needs stitches."

Adam grimaced. They contemplated that, in silence—that Guillaume was very seriously hurt, that he could *die*, maybe, and even though Will figured that all the kids he knew that he hadn't seen at the meeting, and all the adults that had been on that plane, even though he figured that *they* were all dead, it was different when the guy who could die was right in front of you. When there was a body. All those other deaths were maybes.

"I didn't think I'd ever see Ashton Collins look that worried about another human being," Kevin said, and Will jumped again. He was boxed in; Adam on his left, Kevin on his right. "You remember, Will, when we were playing that charter school and that kid broke his leg? Collins was *laughing*."

Will remembered that game. The kid's bone had broken so bad it had been sticking out of the skin. Will remembered a couple kids puking.

And, yeah, he remembered Ashton Collins laughing.

"I mean, Guillaume's no saint," Kevin said. "You remember in pre-K when he used to pull the wings off flies and drop them all in his water bottle? He used to swirl it around and watch them spin."

Will nodded and thought about Sage muttering that Guillaume dying might not be a bad thing.

"They're kids," Adam said. "Just like us. They're not evil. And Guillaume's *hurt*."

"I kinda wanna jump!" Efrain yelled, and when they glanced over at him on the other side of Kevin, a few feet away, he'd stripped down to his briefs, his legs skinny and paler than the rest of him. He was at the edge of the cliff, looking over. "It looks *deep*!"

"Ef, don't," Adam said. "We don't *know*."

"I mean, if we look at how the water from the waterfall's falling," Nicky said. "We can probably approximate—"

Kevin pushed Efrain.

One minute, Efrain was standing at the top of the waterfall with them, the next, his arms were wind-milling in the air and he was screaming. He hit the water hard on his stomach with a massive *splash!* and then it was silent. They stared down at the water. Will could hear his heart pounding in his ears. Kevin looked semi-surprised with himself.

Then they saw Efrain bob to the surface, waving his arms wildly.

"Well," Kevin said. "It's deep."

×

Eventually, they all jumped from the waterfall, even Richard Ayers, and after some time swimming and dunking each other—Kevin and Efrain wrestled in the shallows until Efrain, who probably weighed about half as much as Kevin, accidentally jabbed a heel into Kevin's testicles and Kevin, after recovering, held him underwater so long that Adam almost went over and intervened.

"God, I'm *starved*," Efrain said. Will was hungry, too; it felt like it had been forever since they'd last eaten. "We shoulda raided those suitcases before coming. I know I packed Mike'n'Ikes."

They were all stretched out on the little sandy beach next to the pool at the bottom of the waterfall, except for

Richard Ayers, who was up exploring somewhere. That kid never got tired, it seemed like; then again, he also never really seemed to want to do anything except explore and look at bugs. Unlike Guillaume Argot, when Richard looked at bugs, he seemed to really *like* them; he'd let them crawl on his hands and stuff, and when they'd been in elementary school, he'd used to cry if people squashed them.

"Maybe there's fruit trees or something," Nicky said. Nicky was short and broad-shouldered, with a little potbelly. "You know, to eat."

"Or stuff to hunt," Kevin suggested. "Birds and stuff."

"Guillaume had a knife," Will said. "Like, *on* him. Ashton showed it to us when we were wrapping up his leg. We could use that to hunt stuff once everyone's up here."

They contemplated this, chewed on it a little. Will did wonder why Guillaume had a knife, and how he'd gotten it onto the plane, especially when it had definitely been *on* him, if he'd had it when he crashed. He wondered if maybe that was what had cut his knee open. Not a rock.

But that didn't make any sense. Why would he cut *himself*?

"We could always eat Laurence," Efrain cracked, eventually, and they all laughed, the stress broken, briefly, when Richard Ayers called from up near the waterfall:

"*Guys!* There's a cave back here!"

. chapter five .

The cave behind the waterfall was spacious, and dark, and echoed. "*Hello!*" Efrain called, and when it echoed back to him, he laughed, and when that echoed back to him, he started saying every curse word he knew, at least until Kevin thumped him on the back of the head and told him to, in no uncertain terms, knock it the fuck off.

"This would be a good camp," Adam said. He'd given Kevin an appreciative look, which Will hadn't expected; Adam and Kevin had *never* gotten along. But maybe, Will figured, if Kevin could keep Efrian in line at a time like this, Adam would like him a little bit more. Will had always figured that Efrain and Adam were friends, but maybe there was only so much of Efrain Foley a guy could take.

"So, good news, bad news it, then?" Kevin said. "Bad news, it is an island, good news, we found a camp?"

"I guess," Adam said.

Kevin and Adam grinned at each other, then, in a way that Will had never seen before. While the two were both athletic and both pulled decent enough grades, Kevin was mean. And Adam wasn't. That may have seemed like a nominal difference, but it made one. Kevin was always trying to play catch-up to Adam.

Still, Will figured, if they could get along for this, that would probably be for the best.

×

They made it back to the beach area later that day, and Adam blew his trumpet again to get everyone collected. Will found Sage and dropped to sit beside him. Nearby—Guillaume and Ashton. Guillaume looked barely conscious and enfevered.

"How is he?" Will asked.

"Bad," Sage said. "We found some Tylenol and real bandages, but I didn't want to waste our bottled water on it in case there wasn't any freshwater for drinking."

"There is," Will said. "We found—"

But then Adam started talking, and Will figured that he could tell the story a little better, anyway. Adam sketched through everything—bad news, island, good news, waterfall—and at the end, he looked around at all of them like he was expecting them to tell him what they wanted next.

Laurence Dale raised his hand and Adam called on him like they were in school.

"When are we moving up there?" he asked. "And what about food?"

"It's a little bit of a hike," Adam said. "And someone'll need to help Ashton with Guillaume. So we'll start out tomorrow morning. As for food… did you guys find much in the luggage?"

"Snacks, mostly," Luca Cooke said. "We piled them up over there. We didn't want to eat them all before you got back."

Luca Cooke was somewhat of an anomaly at their school; athletic, but didn't care enough for sports to ever put in enough effort to join, and smart, but again, it was the effort that kicked him away from the honor roll. What he *could* do was make things with his hands. If there was a project that required building or putting something together, Luca was who you wanted on your side. Will wondered if that extended to the culinary arts.

"Luca, would you be in charge of food for us?" Adam asked. "You could grab a couple guys... the twins, maybe, to help you out. Reuben, Briggs, you okay with that?"

"Yeah," said one of the twins—Will couldn't tell them apart—and the other one snapped off a salute.

"Is that okay, Luca? Do you want to?"

"Sure," Luca said. "So, what? Are we going to hunt for food, or..."

"There are animals on the island," Richard Ayers said, from directly next to Will, and Will jumped; he hadn't seen or heard the guy sneaking up. "Big enough to eat, if you want to. And there's fruit trees. So we should be able to survive."

"Anyone know how to hunt?" Adam asked.

"I hunted before," Ryan Spencer said. "But it was with a gun."

They digested that, for a minute.

"We could make spears?" Caleb Smith suggested.

"How, with a sharp rock?" Kevin snapped.

"Guillaume has a knife," Will said, again—Kevin should've known that—and Ashton's face whipped around to glare. Will stood up, a little uncomfortable. "Guillaume has a knife. I guess Ashton has it now. Right? Or Sage?"

"I have it," Ashton muttered. He stood up, all loose-limbed and ready for a fight, like he usually looked. "But when Gill gets better—it's his knife. He gets it back."

"Let me see it," Kevin said, wading through the crowd and Ashton, after glowering at him for a few moments, handed it over. Kevin flicked it open and whistled. "Holy crap. Is this even legal?"

"I dunno," Ashton said. "It's not mine."

"We could hunt with this," Kevin said. He sounded excited, and then glanced back at Adam. "Hey, Nicholson—you think I could grab a couple guys and we could like, hunt? For meat? That could be what we do?"

"Yeah," Adam said. "That would be fine. Pick who you want."

"Yeah! Uh, Ashton, I guess, and Guillaume when he gets better—Will, you too—Ryan, Vic, Leo, Seth—Sawyer—um, anyone else want to?"

Will noticed that everyone Kevin had said, with the exception of Guillaume, was a football player. Even Ashton, who was looking relatively less sulky now that he'd been singled out in some way, played football.

"Jaxson and Tyler. Okay."

"Awesome," Adam said. "And… Nicky, you made us a fire last night. So when we get up there, you're in charge of the fire. You can work with Luca with the food, and… look. This is kind of serious."

It quieted, a little. Will sat down again, next to Sage, who half-heartedly kicked his ankle.

"I don't know if anyone knows where we are," Adam said. "I mean, we had the plane, and obviously there's like, GPS and stuff in there, but who knows where that is right now? And even if they do have some kind of signal showing where we are, it'll take them a while to pinpoint it. So… what we need to do, I think, is have some kind of signal fire. When we go up to the waterfall you'll see, at the top there's a great place for something like that."

"A signal fire?" Kevin said doubtfully. "Would that even do anything?"

Adam shrugged, his color rising a little in his cheeks. "It might be enough to have the cooking fire," he mumbled. "It was just an idea. C'mon. Let's go."

PRESIDENT: Adam

DOCTOR: Sage

FOOD: Luca, Reuben, Briggs

HUNTING: Kevin, Ashton, Guillaume, Will, Ryan, Vic, Leo, Seth, Sawyer, Jaxson, Tyler

FIRE: Nicky

FRUIT: Erik, Cullen, Elian, Cody, Zach, Jeff, Liam, Cameron, Richard (anyone seen him lately?)

SUITCASES: Efrain, Steven, Johnny, Jayden, Tommy, Alfonso

INTERIOR DECORATION: Laurence, Charlie, Billy, Connor, Caleb

SIGNAL (SPELL SOMETHING WITH ROCKS???): Jonathan, Terrell, Callum, Lucas, Tyler

. chapter six .

"What does 'interior decoration' mean?" Will asked Sage, who had written up the list. Sage had a lot of spare time while he made sure Guillaume didn't actually die, which mostly consisted of Sage sitting nearby and trying to give him Tylenol every six hours. Ashton hovered, a lot, when he could, but Kevin was starting to take them out hunting and he couldn't be by Guillaume's side as often as he wanted.

"Basically building beds and stuff. And like, laundry and cleaning," Sage said. "I put Laurence first 'cause he talks like he's in charge or whatever. He's always ordering the guys around. There's going to be some kind of revolt before too long. I heard Billy and Connor talking bout pushing him off the waterfall."

"Kevin pushed Efrain off the waterfall and he's fine," Will said. Efrain and his guys had spent the past couple of days dragging all the suitcases up to the waterfall; they'd been semi-ransacked by the first go-through, but Efrain and them had shoved everything back inside to easier transport them. Once emptied, any first aid stuff went to Sage, food went to Luca, and clothes were organized by size. Some of the guys had balked—and Will had found a shirt of his, a *Linkin Park* shirt, that he'd surreptitiously swapped his uniform shirt with when he'd seen it—but Adam had explained that they needed to share everything. "How's Guillaume?"

Sage shrugged. "Still cooking his brain," he said. Guillaume woke up periodically but he never made any sense; Sage was washing out his wound a few times a day, but he still seemed fevered and sick. "Asks for Ashton all the time. At least I think that's what he wants. Hard to tell sometimes."

Efrain hurried up to them, then, arms full. "Sage!" he said. "I found medicine stuff. Look."

He dumped it on the ground in front of them. Sage sorted through. "Hydrogen peroxide... well, that would've helped Guillaume if he'd gotten it right when he'd cut his stupid knee open... oh, shit."

"What is it?" Efrain asked. He'd mellowed out, a little, in the past couple of days; being shunted to the side had done it to him, Will thought. He'd almost gone from class clown to butt of the joke—or he would have, if Laurence hadn't existed.

"Someone had antibiotics," Sage said. He glanced at Guillaume, who did have his eyes open. They were hazy. He was moving his lips but no words were coming out. "That might... be worth... trying..."

"What if it kills him?" Will asked.

"Well, his leg will anyway, so," Sage said. "I figure. I just... where's Ashton?"

"Out with Kev, I think," Will said. "He takes us out in shifts."

"Let me know when he comes back," Sage said. "I can't ever get Guillaume to eat anything."

×

Will grabbed Ashton as soon as he came back. "No fucking luck," Ashton said. He was breathing hard and sweating. "We creep around the stupid island after *birds* and shit, and we never get *anything*, it's so *stupid*, we have these *stupid* spears, and—"

158

"Sage found something that might help Guillaume," Will said. "But he can't get Guillaume to eat anything, so you gotta come help."

Ashton's mouth snapped shut and he twisted out of Will's grip and he was over there before Will could blink. Will saw him and Sage talk, briefly, and then Ashton was cradling Guillaume's head in his arms, and shoving a pill in his mouth. Guillaume tried to spit it out, but Ashton clapped a hand over his mouth.

Will drew closer.

"Gill, you *gotta swallow it*—you gotta, you'll die otherwise—" Ashton looked around wildly. "You got water?"

Sage scooped up some from the pool with his hands and presented it. They filtered it through Ashton's fingers into Guillaume's mouth. Guillaume's body convulsed, a little; he was trying to throw up.

"You might have to stick your fingers in," Will said. "To push the pill down."

"He'll bite me," Ashton said. Still, he poked his fingers in, briefly, teasing the pill down. He yelped. "*Ow*— Gill, stop it—"

"French him," Ryan Spencer called from the other side of the camp; he'd come back with Ashton. Sage shot him the bird. Ashton, gritting his teeth, pushed the pill farther down Guillaume's throat.

Guillaume's throat rippled and Ashton pulled his hand out. His fingers were bleeding. "Shit," he muttered. He stuck them in his mouth.

Sage handed him the hydrogen peroxide. "You might want to wash those off."

×

When Will went to sleep that night, he slept just a few feet away from Sage, who slept just a few feet away from Ashton and Guillaume. Guillaume, being sick, had been able to wrangle one of the few sleeping bags they'd found. Ashton had piled in with him and clutched him like a teddy bear.

    The next morning, Guillaume's fever had broken.

×

Will woke up early. He always did. It was hard to sleep in on the island. Even if you *wanted* to, there was always so much to *do*. Kevin only took two or three guys out at a time, because there wasn't really anything big enough to warrant more than three or four guys and, anyway, too many of them made too much noise, and the rest of the time, Will helped Sage or Efrain.

    That morning, he woke up earlier than most. He pushed himself up and eased himself out of the cave. It was possible to get out without getting absolutely soaked, but most of the guys jumped through the waterfall anyway. It was almost like a shower. A really, really cold one, but a shower nonetheless.

    The fire was outside. Nicky always stayed up to make sure it stayed lit; during the day, everyone threw in pieces of wood or whatever else they had on hand to keep it going, but Nicky stoked it at night. Will had the idea that he liked being up when nobody else was.

    Guillaume was awake. He sat by the fire. He had a box of something clutched in his hands, and when Will got closer, he saw that they were Dots. "Where'd you get those?" Will asked.

Guillaume jerked his head toward the cave.

"Did Luca give 'em to you?"

Guillaume gave him a look, and Will decided to stop asking questions about the Dots. When Guillaume *looked* at you like that, with those big fucking bags under his eyes that were already scary enough, all deep and dark like a doll's eyes, like a *shark's* eyes, it was best to shut up or find thumbtacks in your shoes.

Will sat down across from him. Nicky was busying himself with making sure there was a decent pile of firewood for the day—and, Will figured, staying away from Guillaume on purpose. "How are you feeling?"

Guillaume shrugged. He ate a Dot. Will's mouth watered when he saw the Dots. All he'd eaten the last four days had been whatever fruit everyone had found and the miniscule serving of snack food Luca gave everyone every day. Efrain and his guys had started going farther out across the island, just in case more suitcases had landed somewhere else, but there wasn't much in terms of real food. Will was pretty sure Luca just opened a bag or a box every day and split it into forty-some equal servings.

"Where's Ashton?"

Guillaume jerked his head toward the cave again.

"Oh," Will said.

It was quiet. Will wanted to leave but didn't really know *how*; eventually, he muttered something about having to go to the bathroom and tromped away through the trees. He guessed that was a normal interaction for Guillaume. He *guessed*. The guy had just been all delirious and fevered for a while. Will had sat by him with Sage. Will had sat there when he cried and asked for Ashton.

But now he was fine. Back to normal.

Will *guessed*.

×

Adam called them together later that day. Will had gone out hunting with Kevin, Leo, and Vic, and like always, they'd come back with nothing. Will got the idea that Kevin was really smarting about the fact that they hadn't gotten anything; also, Will figured, because Guillaume had taken his knife back.

Will dropped to sit next to Sage, who didn't seem to have much to do now that Guillaume was better.

"Right," Adam said. His face was flushed with the effort of blowing his trumpet, and he cleared his throat. "So. I figured we should meet and see how we're all doing."

"How we're all *doing*?" Ashton said. "We're stuck on an island."

"I mean—with our jobs, and everything," Adam said. "Er. Sage?"

"Well, Guillaume's no longer dying," Sage said. "And we have hydrogen peroxide now. So if you have a cut, come to me and I'll wash it out, or you might die."

"Luca?"

"Stop stealing the food," Luca said. "I *know* we had more, because I made a list, and I swear to God, like three boxes of candy disappeared today alone. We can't afford to just eat that stuff whenever we want."

Will glanced over at Guillaume. Guillaume stared back at him dispassionately.

"Kevin?"

Kevin scowled. "We suck," he said. "End of story. And anyway, I don't see why we can't just eat the candy now. It's not like—I mean, just split it up between us. Let us eat it at our own pace."

"No," Luca said. "This way we won't eat it all at *once*, but if people keep stealing—"

"If people keep stealing, then we won't get *any*," Kevin said. "And let me tell you, it's hard to have the energy to hunt when all you've eaten are those crappy tiny bananas and three Swedish Fish."

Adam cleared his throat. "Um. Okay. Um. Nicky? How's the fire?"

Nicky gave a thumbs up.

"Erik?"

"We found coconuts today," Erik said. "They're hard to get, though. Jeff almost broke his leg. Also, we lost Ayers. None of us have seen him in like, days. Figured you might want to know."

"Oh. Um. Yeah, that… if anyone's seen Richard…" Adam trailed off. Everyone looked around at each other. Nobody *had* seen Richard. Will tried to remember the last time he'd talk to the guy and couldn't.

Adam shook himself out of it.

"Efrain? How's the suitcases?"

"All the ones that landed on the beach are up here and organized," Efrain said. "We're looking for other ones." Then he sat down. Adam blinked at him, like he hadn't actually expected Efrain to just give a report and sit down. Efrain was looking rough, Will thought. He looked haggard, and nervous, and jumpy.

It probably didn't help that Kevin and Ryan Spencer kept sneaking up on him and scaring him every chance they got. There was some kind of pecking order to the jobs, and hunters were on top, and while the suitcase guys weren't as kicked around as Laurence's guys, they definitely weren't *cool*.

"Laurence? How's the cave coming? Did you figure out laundry?"

Laurence Dale, a self-important kid who really didn't seem to do much other than complain, sat up and puffed out his chest. "We've made some mattresses out of grass," he said. "And of course we have those couple sleeping bags—I know Ashton and Guillaume were sharing one—"

"*Gay*," Ryan Spencer intoned.

"—and if you're willing to share, I honestly don't see why you couldn't have one of the other ones. With a partner."

"We only shared because he was sick," Ashton said. Him and Guillaume were sitting near the other hunters. Ashton was tapping a spear against his foot and his color was rising. "We're not—it's not *gay*, he was *sick*."

"*Okay*," Adam said. "Jonathan? Signal?"

Jonathan shrugged. "We started spelling HELP with rocks," he said. "But then we realized that the rocks were the same color as the ground at the top of the waterfall. So now we're looking for rocks that aren't gray."

"Okay," Adam said. "Um, if any of you guys, when you're out, find something they could use to spell, let us know. Okay? That's probably everything. Luca, when'll supper be ready?"

Luca shrugged. "I dunno. Couple minutes, maybe. I just gotta see what we have and split it up."

. chapter seven .

"I *got* one!"

Kevin's voice was high-pitched, almost shrieking, and Will jerked his head up. They'd been hunting, again, trying to throw wooden sticks at birds that flew almost before they had their arm pulled back, at squirrels that would sit still long enough to make you think you had it, and at rabbits that teased them with how fat they looked. But Kevin, now, was brandishing a rabbit. He held it by the ears.

Will hurried over. Guillaume and Ashton— Guillaume still limping, a little—joined them. "You gonna kill it?" Ashton asked. "Did you even hurt it?"

"I thought it might work better if I just tried to catch it first," Kevin said. His color was high. He was grinning. "And it *did*!"

"It's not dead yet, though," Ashton said.

Kevin glanced around at them. "The knife?" he said.

Guillaume handed over the knife. Kevin held it awkwardly in his free hand like he wasn't sure what to do with it.

"Where do I…"

"I'll do it," Ashton said, grabbing the knife and, before anyone could move, slashing it straight across the rabbit's neck. Blood spurted, splashing him like some kind of slasher villain, and Kevin screamed and dropped the rabbit. It died on the forest floor, its back feet kicking a little. "Anyone know how to skin these, or can we just sort of make it up as we go along?"

He glanced around. Will took a step back. Guillaume, though, seemed entranced. He took a step forward. Traced the blood on Ashton's face. Ashton dropped to his knees. Will felt like he was intruding on some kind of private moment; the kid of moment you walked in on your mom and dad having when you were supposed to be asleep.

He took another step back.

"We'll figure it out," Guillaume said. "I read about it in books."

"Okay," Ashton said. Guillaume's hand was still on his face, but he didn't seem to mind. They were only looking at each other.

"You can't just—" Kevin started, and then shook his head and, apparently seeing that Will was the only sane one around, changed course and headed for him. "Am I nuts, or was that creepy?"

"It was, uh," Will tried to think of a word that wouldn't set Ashton and Guillaume after him while he slept. "Sudden."

"It was insane, is what it was," Kevin said.

"But we have meat," Will pointed out.

"I guess," Kevin said. "One rabbit, but if we keep catching them with our hands and…"

"And, what?" Ashton said. "I have to keep killing them 'cause all of you are too big of pussies to do it yourselves?"

"I could kill a rabbit," Guillaume said. He was still wiping blood from Ashton's face. They were both on their knees by now. The rabbit had really sprayed everywhere.

"I know *you* could," Ashton said.

"We could split you guys up," Will said. "One of you—"

"No," Guillaume said. He glanced up, met Will's eyes, and Will took a step back. It was the most emotion he'd ever seen in Guillaume's eyes, that was for sure, and it was anger. "We're staying together."

"Okay," Will said. His voice cracked.

"Let's head back," Kevin said. "This is the most luck we've ever had, so—let's just head back now."

×

With about forty kids, nobody got much more than half a mouthful, but the bit that they *did* get, Will figured, still sucking on his fingers to try and get every last bit of fat, was the best thing he'd ever tasted. Ashton was certainly hamming it up. Guillaume was at his side, but everyone was talking to him; he'd gone over how he'd killed the rabbit probably about six times, each time talking louder, gesturing more wildly, and grinning wider. By virtue of being on the hunt, Will had gotten a little bit of fame. Not much, but a little.

"Did it really happen like that?" a voice asked, and Will glanced back. It was Efrain.

"What?" Will said.

"Like he's saying," Efrain said. He looked thinner; of course, they all did. Even Laurence Dale, who had plenty to spare, was starting to get thinner. "Did he actually rib its throat out with his teeth?"

"Is *that* what he's saying now?" Will said. "No. Kevin caught it but froze up when it came to killing it, and Ashton took the knife and cut its throat. Then Guillaume got a little weird about the blood."

"Oh," Efrain said. He snorted. "Is it insane that I actually believed that he'd ripped a rabbit's throat out with his teeth?"

"Not really," Will said. "He's a creep."

Efrain nodded a few times and then sat down. Wrapped his knees up in his arms and shivered. Will noticed a bruise on his cheek; dark, streaking across his flesh like someone had hit him with a branch or something.

"What happened to your face?"

"Huh?" Efrain said.

Will pointed.

"Oh," Efrain said. "Uh. Tripped."

"Oh," Will said. He didn't know if he believed Efrain, but what else was he supposed to think? Someone was hurting people? If it got to that point they were all well and truly fucked. Will thought of how Guillaume had acted when Ashton had stood with blood on his face. How Ashton had dropped to his knees immediately.

He shivered a little and forgot about it. He didn't want to worry about shit like that. Not on the island. Shit was creepy, sometimes, and he *knew* that; he sure didn't want to fucking think about it.

. chapter eight .

Another meeting.

It was during these meetings that Will realized how bad they all *stank*. When they all gathered together in a way that they rarely did otherwise, other than sleeping—well, they were forty or so unwashed preteen boys wearing clothes that couldn't even pretend to be clean. Supposedly Laurence and his guys did laundry, but that mostly meant that every four or so days one of them would hand you a different set of clothes to put on.

Some guys (Will included) tried to do their own laundry, but they didn't have soap. Plain water, fresh or salt, didn't do much.

It was the same old argument, this meeting. Luca was convinced someone was stealing food (and someone probably was), and then Kevin would jump in and say hunters should get more food, since they *provided* food; and it was true, of course, that they were bringing in more meat now. They were actually getting semi-good at it. Will had killed a bird the other day. Caught it in a net Efrain had made him from a piece of parachute and then headed over and snapped its neck. It wasn't enough meat by far—everyone was starting to look as emaciated as Guillaume these days—but it was more than they'd been getting. As well as that, the scavengers were getting good at figuring out where the most fruit was.

"I know who it is," Guillaume said, and Luca stared at him, mouth half-open. Will wondered if he was going to confess. Will was about seventy percent sure that Guillaume was the one stealing.

"Who?" Luca said, finally.

"Who do you fucking think?" Guillaume asked. His voice was quiet, and it grew quieter the more he talked. He was picking at his fingernails. In terms of 'things Guillaume didn't do,' 'talk to a whole group of people at once' was pretty high on the list. "Who's the fattest guy here?"

They all looked at Laurence, who got very red, very fast. The problem was—and Will barely had time to think about this, before everything kept going, faster and faster and faster until it was impossible to stop—was that whether Laurence was stealing the food or not, he was going to look guilty. Laurence was the unfortunate combination of someone who couldn't take conflict and inspired it just by being himself. "I'm—I'm not *stealing* anything—"

"Then why are you still so fat?" Ashton asked, jumping in, and Guillaume faded back into his comfortable position as Ashton's shadow. "Why aren't you getting skinny like the rest of us?"

"I—I *have* lost weight, I just, I—" Laurence was stumbling now.

"Face it, Dale," Ashton jeered. "You're a fucking pig. You can't handle being hungry and so you're taking from the rest of us when *really*, we shouldn't even be feeding you. You're already too fat. I'm pretty sure it runs in your family, right?"

"Nobody runs in his family," Ryan Spencer yelled.

Ashton grinned at him, briefly; a flit of an expression across his face, before he kept going. He was pushing, and pushing, and pushing—and Laurence was getting more than embarrassed. He was getting mad. "Didn't your dad die of a heart attack because he was so fat? Didn't your mom just get that fat people surgery, the one—"

Laurence charged.

Say one thing about Laurence Dale: when he got moving—that mass was something to behold. Ashton Collins, who was tall but skinny, didn't have a chance. He got absolutely laid out. Laurence was sobbing and yelling and sitting on his chest, and Ashton was turning purple, and then, before any of them could do anything, Guillaume's knife was sticking out of Laurence's back.

Twelve times.

By the end, Laurence was still on the ground, and Ashton was breathing hard, his eyelids fluttering.

Guillaume knelt beside Laurence's body and pulled out the knife.

"Holy shit," Adam said. "Holy shit. Holy shit, he's dead."

Guillaume nodded and wiped off the knife. He glanced up. "He coulda killed Ash," he said. "Right?"

"I—I *guess*," Adam said. He looked absolutely bewildered. Will glanced sideways at Sage, who was wide-eyed and pale. Trembling. Slightly.

"And now we don't have to share with him. Food, I mean," Guillaume said. He hesitated. And then he said something that Will didn't get for a few moments. "People are made of meat."

They were silent. Ashton pushed himself up onto his elbows and wiped at his face.

Luca was the first one who got it. That, or he was the first one who was willing to say something. "No. No way. We're not—we're not eating Laurence. We're not—"

"We can't live on four or five rabbits a day," Guillaume said. "I'll butcher him. Ashton will help."

"He will?" Ashton said. His voice cracked and it did make Will feel a little better that he seemed just as freaked as everyone else.

"Won't you?"

Ashton's throat rippled. He didn't say anything.

Guillaume sighed and stood up. Turned around to face the majority of them. They all moved back in a ripple, like a wave before a tsunami, and Guillaume spoke. It was the most Will had ever heard Guillaume say at one time, and he said it all as dispassionately as he'd ever said anything.

"Look: we're going to starve to death. Coconuts and bananas and a mouthful of meat if we're lucky isn't going to keep us alive. There are way too many of us. I didn't kill him on purpose. I only killed him because he coulda killed Ash. But now we've got one less mouth to feed and he can feed us. I know it was my kill, so I'll butcher him and we can cook him and we can pretend he's pork or something."

"Can't you go nuts from eating someone?" Cameron Riley asked. His voice was shaky. "Can't you get like—diseases?"

"Not if it's cooked well," Guillaume said. He leveled a look at Luca, who was still shaking his head. "Luca. It's your job to cook."

"It's not—it's not my job to cook *people*," Luca said. His voice was strangled. "I can't cook *people*."

"I bet you can," Guillaume said. Then he knelt down and started to cut the clothes of off Laurence, right then, right there, and everyone stood up at once. He was going to do this right here, right now—thank God, Will thought, that they didn't have their meetings inside. It was out around the fire, but *at least they weren't inside.*

Will glanced around and just caught Sage as he beat a fast track out of there. He tried to catch up to him, pushing through the crowd, and caught Sage puking behind a tree. "Sage," he said. "You good?"

"*No*," Sage said. His voice was rough and when he looked up Will saw that he was crying. "I'm not—I'm *not* okay, that—the way he did that, that was, he was just, he was just like, he was—"

"I get it," Will said, and Sage nodded a few times, and then he stuck his head back behind the tree and puked again. Will, not knowing what else to do, sort of just rubbed his back. Sage seemed so fragile under his T-shirt. "I mean… I mean, Laurence really coulda killed Ashton. If nobody did anything."

Sage shrugged.

"And Guillaume is… a whole lot littler than him," Will said. Part of him realized, dimly, that he was really trying to justify it all to himself, but he could figure out how to make himself stop. "I mean… maybe he thought the knife was the only way to get him off."

"Maybe," Sage said. He sniffed and wiped at his face with the back of his hand. He gagged again, but nothing came up. "Are you… are you gonna…"

"Eat him?"

Sage nodded.

"I dunno," Will said. "Probably not, I guess."

×

But God it smelled good.

Will didn't know how Guillaume had convinced Luca to start cooking Laurence, but Kevin was there, watching everything, and Luca had a brand new black eye, and Adam was watching all of this from the outskirts of the group, bemused, horrified, and Will wandered over to him. "What happened?"

Adam shrugged, and then he let out some kind of laugh. "I don't think I'm the president anymore," he said. "I—I tried to tell him to stop, to—he just kept cutting, Will. He just kept cutting, and then Kevin started ordering the other hunters to help, and Luca—Luca *wouldn't*, but Ryan and some of the other guys held him down and—I mean, you can see his *face*, that's just what shows—I tried to talk to Kevin, but he said—he said there's no point in wasting the meat."

"It smells good," Will said, and immediately he wished he could take it back, because Adam flinched and then said, with some kind of new venom,

"I *know*. That's the worst part."

There was a pile of innards over by Laurence's clothes, and bones, and Guillaume, who was still carving. He was going at it like a science dissection. He tossed aside things he didn't think he needed. Ashton was standing over him, dancing from foot to foot. He looked uncomfortable. Will wondered if the other guys were only comfortable, or at least semi-comfortable, because they could pretend it wasn't Laurence.

Like his glasses, like his *head*, wasn't in the pile of innards.

Will felt vomit rise up and forced it back down. "Are you gonna eat?" he asked.

Adam shrugged. "I dunno," he said. He shivered and hugged himself, clutching at his elbows, and rocked back on his heels. "Probably. I'm hungry."

Will nodded a few times.

"First meat's up!" Kevin yelled.

Nobody moved. Everyone stayed where they were, like they didn't want to be the first one, and eventually, Guillaume elbowed Ashton.

"Oh," Ashton said. "Right."

He went up. He took the meat. It was easier to think of it like that, like *meat*, not like Laurence. And then Ashton took a bite. After he took the first bite it was like it was all over; they all watched in silent horror as he devoured it, like a dog that hadn't been fed in days. When he was done, he looked around at all of them, wiped off his mouth with the back of his hand and said, his voice small, "It's good."

They all started going for it, then, and that was the night that Will had his first taste of human flesh.

It wasn't his last.

. chapter nine .

Laurence lasted them a long time, but not long enough.
    Luca cooked him well, and after a while—especially after Kevin made the housekeepers cart away his head and clothes and everything—it was easy to forget that he was a person. Had been a person. Will ate with the rest of them, and he had to admit: it was good.
    It was good.
    He hoped that it was just hunger saying that.
    Too, Will was noticing something awful and terrifying: Adam was president when he called meetings, but more and more people were going to Kevin to solve their problems. Will even found himself doing it. And Kevin's answers were rarely what Adam would have said. Once James Howard said that Efrain was making fun of him and Kevin had said, "We'll take care of it." Then Ryan Spencer held Efrain's head underwater, dunked him over and over, until Efrain was gasping and sobbing and apologizing.
    And Adam didn't do anything about it.
    Sage was busier than ever. It was like every day there were three or four kids going to him with cuts, with arms they thought were broken—all kinds of 'accidents.' Sage would patch them up the best he could, but he was running low on supplies. He started to look haunted. To get jumpy. Richard Ayers stayed gone, but at this point, Will wondered if maybe he was the smart one. If he was surviving on whatever fruit he was finding and just… hanging out.
    That is, if he was still alive.

Will watched it all as someone on the outside looking in. As a hunter, he was left pretty well alone. He went out, he caught birds and rabbits; once or twice he found nests of eggs that he'd bring back to Luca, who would nod half-heartedly and cook them. Luca was getting good at cooking things; before, at the beginning, everything came out sort of charred, but Luca was getting it together.

Those were the ones that were the jumpiest: Efrain, Sage, and Luca. Oh, sure, Will was sure that some of the other guys were getting rough. But those were the three he knew the best and they were getting the shit kicked out of them practically constantly. When Cullen McCray died, in an 'accident,' Kevin said, while very much not looking at Guillaume and Ashton, who were curiously clean, like they'd taken a quick dip to wash off before coming back to camp, and it was a waste not to use the meat, Luca had refused to cook again.

And gotten pummeled again.

Adam was in charge in name only.

It was the kind of shit that got kind of scary, sometimes.

It was nighttime, time to sleep—generally, the only person up at night was Nicky, tending to the fire—and Will was heading to his usual place next to Sage when Ryan Spencer waved him over. Will frowned and changed course.

"Dude, you gotta start sleeping over here with us," Ryan said. "See how we're all kind of split up by job?"

Will glanced around the cave. Sure, everyone was sleeping by people they worked with... but that was mostly, Will figured, because they were friends. Will's best friend was Sage, and he said so.

"Yeah, and Sage is fine," Ryan said. "Like, he can patch you up if you fall down or whatever. But you gotta start staying with us. You can be *friends* with him or whatever, but you gotta hang out more with us. We're a *team*."

Will glanced at Kevin, who was picking at his fingernails, and Kevin shrugged.

"Guillaume and Ashton don't sleep with you guys," Will said.

"Yeah, well," Ryan said. "They're close by."

Guillaume and Ashton didn't sleep with anyone but each other—they were near-ish to the hunters, but far enough away that you couldn't hear what they were saying when they whispered to each other late at night. Far enough away that when they snuck out at night they wouldn't wake anyone up.

"Also, they're creeps," Will said.

Ryan shrugged. He glanced sideways at them—they were doing their whispering routine, sitting with their backs against the wall. Guillaume was tracing Ashton's kneecap with his knife. Ashton was just letting it happen. It hit Will then that Ryan was *scared* of them—Ryan, who could probably take any one of them in the cave without breaking a sweat. If *Ryan Spencer* was *afraid* of them—

Will cut his thoughts off.

"Look," Ryan said. "If you aren't with us, you're against us. And you see what happens to the guys that are against us, right?"

Will thought about Efrain Foley bawling his eyes out by the pool, soaking wet and shivering. Luca Cooke cooking human flesh, his face puffy with bruises, moving slow. Laurence Dale and a knife going in and out of his back twelve times. "I guess," Will said.

"Like I said," Ryan said. "Sage is fine and all to hang out with and whatever. But you gotta sleep over here with us now."

×

Adam called a meeting the next morning, before the first set of hunters went out. They all filed dutifully out of the cave. Adam put his trumpet down, cleared his throat, and said, face red, "I'm stepping down as president."

"*What?*" Efrain Foley said, jerking to his feet. For a minute he was the old Efrain again; the kid who cut up in class and made people laugh and had more energy than he knew what to do with. The kid who was semi-bullheaded and would say what was on his mind, damn the consequences. "You can't do that, Adam, all these other guys *suck*."

"Watch it, Foley," Kevin rumbled, and Efrain jumped and he was scared-Efrain again. Island-Efrain.

"I don't..." Adam trailed off, looking around at them. He looked helpless. "Look, none of you guys are even... you don't even really *listen* to me anymore. I don't think I'm really the leader anymore. So I'm just like. Making it official, I guess. I'll join up with anyone who wants me."

"I think that's a stupid idea," Luca said. His voice cut through the early morning air like Guillaume's knife. He was holding his side and scowling. "You stop and those of us who aren't hunters will be even more second-class citizens. You know we haven't gotten fruit in days? The fruit guys keep going hunting. The fire was out three days in a row because Nicky went hunting instead of—"

"I did *not*—" Nicky started, but Luca bulldozed him and kept going.

"—instead of staying up to watch it. I had to chase him down so I could cook. The only people who don't run off and hunt when they're not supposed to are Sage and the twins and Efrain. Sometimes I think Richard had the right idea, getting out of here right away. That is if he's not dead too. If he's not some of the meat that they keep bringing me."

"Only Laurence and Cullen are dead," Kevin said. "That's it. Nobody else. Ayers just ran off because he's autistic or something and doesn't like people."

"Whatever," Luca said. He sat down, hard, on the ground, and crossed his arms.

Adam looked lost. "I don't…" he trailed off. "There's nothing I can do. I'll help out around camp, Luca, I will, I won't just run off with the hunters."

"Awesome," Luca said. "Then you can see how they treat us. Spencer swings at me just to make me flinch now, and without me you'd all have like, salmonella."

"Learn to take a joke, Cooke," Ryan Spencer said. "If you didn't flinch every time, it wouldn't be funny."

"If you didn't hit me when I didn't want to cook *people*, I wouldn't flinch," Luca said. He looked near tears. "You guys, are we seriously *doing* this? Do we really *eat people*? Is that what we're doing now?"

It was quiet. Will shifted. He could see Sage across the way. As far as he knew, they weren't really beating up on Sage like they were Luca and Efrain. Sage had a kind of protection that the other two didn't… he was the doctor and, more than that, Will figured, he was close friends with a hunter. An original. Will wondered if that would change now that Will didn't sleep next to him at night anymore.

Either way, Sage looked like he agreed with Luca. But he knew better than to say it. Sage had grown up in a house where saying the wrong thing would get you hurt, and that was serving him well here.

"We only eat them when it's a waste not to," Kevin said, finally, and he slid right into place as the new leader. Will could almost hear the *click* as he shunted Adam aside—like a piece in a puzzle. "Cooke, I get it. I know it sucks to have to cook them. But that's your job. And otherwise we'll starve to death. Do you want to starve to death?"

Luca was breathing hard. "I want everyone else to do their jobs, too," he said. "We need fruit or we'll get diseases. Like, like—scurvy, like pirates."

Kevin nodded a few times. "Sure," he said. He cleared his throat. "But I do think that we need more hunters. So I'm going to take the guys who were going through suitcases and the guys who were making a signal for help. The rest of you guys—"

"I'm not doing it," Efrain said. He sat with his knees pulled up to his chest, his chin perched on them, all folded up protectively. "I'll stick around and help Luca. You can take Laurence's guys, probably. They always go anyway."

Kevin nodded again. "Sure," he said. "So, fruit guys have to be picking fruit, and Luca, the twins, Efrain, Sage, Adam, and Nicky will stick around at camp."

"I could teach these guys how to make a fire," Nicky said. "Then I could come with you guys."

"Sure," Kevin said. "If you can teach them. Also, if anyone's not doing their job, they're getting their ass kicked. No more messing around."

And just like that, the power flipped.

. chapter ten .

With Kevin in charge, it was different.

Will had to admit that more did get done. The fruit guys, after getting thoroughly reamed out and beaten up, were picking fruit again. The people that stayed at the camp worked hard—the twins didn't goof off anymore or anything. Nicky taught everyone how to start a fire, not just the ones who stayed at camp, so that everyone could do it, and then he started hunting, too. And nobody really mouthed off.

Nobody except Efrain.

Kevin didn't call meetings like Adam had. Nothing was a discussion. He didn't ask anyone how it was going. Every morning they met before the hunters went out, Kevin would say what needed to be done that day, any punishments that needed meted out would be meted out, and then everyone would break.

This morning, Kevin went through the list, and everyone was about to break, when Ryan Spencer muscled his way through and chucked Efrain on the ground in front of the fire. Efrain was bruised and bloody and sobbing quietly on his hands and knees. Sage started for him.

"Not yet, Horton," Kevin said. There was something hard in his face—something that Will associated with when they were hunting. When he had a bird or a rabbit in his hands and was getting ready for the kill. "He hasn't been punished yet."

"He hasn't?" Sage said.

Kevin shook his head, and Sage took a step back. Disappeared into the crowd. If he'd pushed it, *maybe*,

Efrain would have survived it. That's what Will thought later, after it was all over. If Sage had pushed... Sage had some influence, as nominal as it was, that maybe they would've just beat him up more. Broken a bone or two.

But Guillaume and Ashton came out. Guillaume and Ashton with the knife.

(Who was the murderer? It was Guillaume and Ashton in front of the fire with the knife. No butler involved.)

Ashton grabbed Efrain. Hoisted him up. Efrain kicked, and struggled, and from his mouth came pleading words, begging words—"*Please*, please, please don't, *please*, I'm *sorry*, I'll go, I'll *go*, I'll leave you *alone*, I'm *sorry, please*."

"This is an example," Kevin said. His face was stone. "We won't survive if we're not together on everything. Foley made too much noise about shit that didn't concern him. This is a warning to all of you. Go ahead, Argot."

Guillaume smiled beautifully. Will had never seen Guillaume smile before, and it lit up his whole face. It almost made him look like someone you might want to be friends with. Efrain was screaming now, wordlessly, and trying to push himself backward with his heels, but Ashton held him. Ashton was skinny but he was *wiry*, and Efrain was just plain skinny. Ashton held him without much effort at all.

Guillaume flicked open the knife and then, without warning, Efrain's guts were on the ground. Efrain was still alive, still screaming, and Ashton dropped him. He curled onto his side and started doing—*something*, and then Will realized that he was trying to put his guts back *in*, and they kept slipping through his fingers. They were *slippery*; Will hadn't known that guts were so *wet*. His screams were breaking off into sobs, broken sobs that devolved into a sort of *gluk-gluk-gluk* sound, and then he laid his head down and he died.

×

It was after Efrain that some of them started talking about running away. Will came back from hunting that day and Sage waved him over. Will went, shaking hair out of his eyes. His hair was getting long. He wondered about maybe asking Guillaume to borrow the knife, *but—*

Sage led him through the trees, to a clearing a ways away, to Luca and the twins and Adam and, amazingly, Richard Ayers.

"You're alive," Will said.

Richard nodded distractedly. He had a few bumps and scrapes; nothing that screamed any sort of foul play, but more like he'd fallen out of trees… which, knowing Richard Ayers, was probably the case.

"What the *fuck* is he doing here?" Luca asked. His voice cracked. He was pacing, twisting his hands back and forth, cracking his knuckles. "He's one of *them*, he can't—you can't—*Sage*—"

"He's one of the good ones," Sage said. He looked at Will, who shrugged. "He's not… he's not a bad person."

It was quiet.

"I hope you know that when he goes and tells his hunter buddies what we're doing, we're all going to die, and it's going to be your fault," Luca said. He let out a long, shuddering breath, and shook his head again. "I'm not cooking Efrain. I'm not *doing* it."

"That's why we're all here," Adam said. Here, in the smaller group, he regained some of his control. He tried out a smile. It was a pale mockery of the grin he'd used to have, but it was something. "Rich, would it be okay if we came and lived with you?"

"I guess," Richard said. "I don't have very much room, but you can, I guess. It's not as nice as the cave."

"Ayers, the middle of the ocean would be nicer than the cave," Luca said. He let out a shuddering breath. "Sage, you never said why he's here."

"Man on the inside," Sage said. He looked sideways at Will. "If you want."

"I—I guess," Will said. He stuttered because he was scared of Guillaume, too, and the thought of what Guillaume would do to him if he found out—

But he was an original hunter. That had to count for something.

"So you want like, information?" Will said. "Food?"

Sage was nodding. Luca was still looking incredulously at him. "Let me ask you something, Black," he said. "Are you guys all just actually fucking insane? Is that why you're following them around?"

Will shrugged.

"We're all going to die here," Luca said. "We're all so fucking dead."

. chapter eleven .

Nobody seemed to care much that a small chunk of people had disappeared. Wounds, without Sage there to bandage them up, went unwashed and unbandaged. That's how Sawyer Hurley went. He got a nasty cut and then it started weeping and swelling and he was hot to the touch and ravaged by fever and then one morning he was dead. Guillaume cut him up and they ate him. Every so often Will would sneak off with an armful of fruit or something and meet with one of the guys from the group—usually Sage, who trusted him, or Richard, who was preternaturally quiet in the trees—and tell them what was going on. If anyone noticed that he was leaving, with food especially, they didn't say anything.

That was Will's superpower, he figured: his ability to go unnoticed. In a situation like this, it wasn't bad.

Elian Larson and Cody Green died in some freak hunting accident. Will didn't know how. He wasn't there. Guillaume and Ashton dragged their bodies back. Cody Green was missing an ear. Will didn't ask how they'd died, not seriously, and he'd partaken in their flesh.

Cameron Riley fell out of a tree and broke his leg. After a few days, his moaning was too much and Guillaume walked over and slit his throat.

Liam Martin drowned.

Jayden May was allergic to coconuts and some of them, somehow, made their way into his food one day.

Tommy Hudson got shoved into the fire and was burned so bad he crisped up. He laid there, shaking, for a few days before giving it up and killing himself with Guillaume's knife, which had found its way near him.

It was after Tommy Hudson that Guillaume and Ashton got a little more creative.

×

Meeting that morning. Kevin was looking strained. He was hardly at camp anymore. He'd go out to hunt, and he'd hunt, for sure, and he was the last one out, and when he came back he hid himself away in the cave and if you wanted to talk to him you had to go through Ryan Spencer, who was some kind of bodyguard. Guillaume and Ashton meted out all the punishment and they were the ones who decided who needed to be on the chopping block.

"Alfonso and Charlie," Kevin said, and Ryan Spencer and Vic Walsh pulled them out. Vic Walsh was too decent of a guy to be involved in this, Will thought dully. He was big and athletic, though, and that was why he was. "They've been talking about escaping. Like those guys that ran out on us after—you know."

After Efrain. It ran through all of their heads like pop music.

Guillaume and Ashton came for them. Will was sitting on the ground, near the fire, next to Nicky, and he watched. It was really all they could do at this point.

Just watch.

"Kevin, please, we didn't do anything—" Alfonso tried, and Ashton hit him in the mouth. He cowered, his arms over his face.

"Do what you need to do," Kevin said, and he turned to the rest of them. "Will, Lucas, Ryan, c'mon. We're going hunting."

"Don't you want us to watch?" Ryan asked.

Kevin shook his head and started for the trees. Will picked himself up and followed. Alfonso and Charlie were screaming but Will didn't want to look back. With a kind of sickness in the pit of his stomach, Will figured that there would be fresh meat tonight whether they caught anything or not.

Will wondered if he should say anything. Wondered if *now* was the time, if now was when he should ask Kevin if he really knew what they were doing, if everything was *really* OK—but the screams stopped him. Even if Kevin didn't hate him for asking, maybe Ryan would. Or Lucas would. They'd tell Guillaume, or Ashton, and then Kevin wouldn't have a choice anymore.

"How many of us are left?" Kevin asked abruptly.

"What?" Will said.

"How many?" Kevin said. "Not counting those guys that disappeared. How many?"

Will shrugged. Thought about it.

"Twenty-four," Lucas said. "I think."

Kevin nodded a few times.

"Why?" Lucas said.

"That's a lot gone," Kevin said. He was blinking furiously, and it hit Will that Kevin didn't want this to happen any more than the rest of them did. But he was caught, Will figured; if he showed weakness… everyone was scared of Guillaume and Ashton. If Kevin kicked them out, they could kill anyone. Now it was at least semi-controlled.

Will wanted to ask Kevin if this was what was going on. If this was why he didn't stop them, why he kept going out hunting, all of that… but if he was *wrong*—

If he was wrong, he'd be next. So he just kept his mouth shut.

×

When they got back to camp, Billy Byers and Connor Berry were dead, too.

. chapter twelve .

With Caleb Smith, Guillaume and Ashton got even more creative. While the other guys had died quick, or in a way that made Will think that they were, maybe, sort of, trying to make it look like they weren't crazy, Caleb Smith was tortured. He was tortured for days. Guillaume and Ashton didn't go anywhere. They didn't go hunting. They hardly ate. They just played with Caleb, giggling a little, while everyone around them tried studiously to ignore them.

Eventually, it ended when Caleb let out a loud scream, one that ripped through his vocal cords like a knife through bread, and he was silent.

"How long was that?" Ashton yelled. "How long did he *scream*?"

If Guillaume answered, Will didn't know. He was off before he could hear, and in the next few moments he was at the place where he usually met the group that had run off. He sat there, his head in his knees, and waited. He didn't care if Luca wanted to chase him off, or thought that he wasn't really on their side—he couldn't be there anymore. He couldn't do it.

Dimly, he realized he was crying. "Fuck," he muttered into his hands. He was shaking. He couldn't stop himself from shaking. Everything felt awful. He felt like he was going to puke.

"Will?"

Will glanced back. There was Sage. "Hey," Will said. His voice cracked. "It's getting really—really fucking bad, back there. They just killed Caleb. They worked at it for days before he—before he just—"

Sage crossed to him and sat beside him and put an arm around his shoulders. He was small, Sage was, but Will curled into him anyway. Put his head on his shoulder and sobbed. "I can't stay there anymore," Will said. "I can't—I mean, it's, he's, it's crazy, there, and Kevin doesn't do anything about it, and—"

"You can come live with us, if you want," Sage said. "I mean—I mean…"

Will let out a long breath. "I have to," he said. "I have to, I won't—I won't *last*—how does Luca feel about it?"

"He'll have to deal," Sage said. "I know other people are looking for us but we keep hidden pretty well, and if he thinks that you'll… I mean, you're different."

Will shrugged. He didn't know that he was really all that different from anyone else, but he wasn't about to deny it when it could get him out of the nutcase camp. "Thanks," he said. He wiped at his face.

"Let's go," Sage said. "I'll show you where we have our camp."

Sage stood up and offered Will a hand. Will took it and let himself get pulled to his feet. He followed Sage, his head down, through trees and brush until eventually they came to a small clearing. The clearing ran up against the hill, but there was nothing special about it. There was nobody there. "It's us," Sage called.

From the trees, Luca's voice: "He's not coming in."

"He's done being with them," Sage said. "He's done. They're getting—it's getting bad."

"Tough shit," Luca called.

"Luca, come *on*. Let us in."

Then the side that ran up the hill began to move, and Luca was on the other side, arms crossed. Behind him was a decently-sized camp. "Did you *build* this?" Will asked.

"Yeah," Luca said, and Will was reminded of how much they'd wasted him making him cook. "Come *in*. I don't want anyone who might've followed him to see."

"Nobody followed me," Will said, but Sage pushed him toward the entrance of the camp. Inside, Adam sat at a small fire. He glanced back at them.

"Hey, Will," he said. He looked haggard, and thin. They all did.

"Where are the twins?" Will asked.

"Collecting some food," Adam said. "We found a patch of berries a ways away and we go and get stuff from there most days. Eggs, too. We found turtle eggs."

"You can eat turtle eggs?" Will asked.

"Well, nobody's died yet," Adam said.

"Now that I'm here, I can hunt," Will said. "Birds and stuff. I…" But it hit him, then, that he didn't have his net or anything. He'd rushed out of there with nothing. Adam seemed to read it on his face and gave him a sympathetic look. "I'm sorry."

"Don't be," Adam said. "It's not your fault. What was your final straw, by the way? Luca says they've been killing like crazy."

Will swallowed. "Caleb took days," he said. "He took… they had… his *skin*, it was…" His stomach lurched and he pressed a hand to his mouth. Tried to keep it down, grimly, and then he remembered what (*who*) was in his stomach and he upchucked.

"Ah, god damn it," Luca said, disgusted. "Not in the fort."

"I'm *sorry*," Will said, and he was crying again. "I'm sorry, I'll clean it up, I'm sorry—" And it hit him, too, that he was better fed, stronger than these guys because of what (*who*) he'd been eating and he upchucked again. He was on his hands and knees now, sobbing, puke between his hands, and he couldn't stop thinking about it, couldn't stop retching—when you were *in* it, when you were there you hardly thought about it. You hardly thought that you were eating Tommy or Alfonso, or Billy, or Jayden.

Efrain.

But now it was all he could think about.

Sage was next to him then, rubbing his back, and Will was sobbing harder. He didn't think it was possible to cry this hard, but he was crying so hard his throat was constricting again, and he couldn't breathe, and *how could he have done it*? Why hadn't he been with these guys from the beginning? Why had he *stayed*?

"I'm sorry," Will said again, but it wasn't really to these guys. It was to Efrain, and Laurence, and all the other ones. "I'm sorry."

He sniffed, tried to get his tears under control, and looked up. Met Adam's eyes.

"We gotta do something."

. chapter thirteen .

Apparently Luca had been arguing for something like this for a while. "The problem is fucking Guillaume," he said. "Guillaume and Ashton. If they weren't there, you'd have Kevin and Ryan beating people up, maybe, but you can't tell me they'd be slaughtering people."

"Kevin hates it," Will said, suddenly, remembering when Kevin had asked how many were left. "He's gone almost all the time. Hunting. All day."

"Great," Luca said. "Easier to get to them."

"Could we find and talk to Kevin, maybe?" Adam said. "Could he be reasoned with?"

But Will shook his head, and Luca snorted and leaned back. "He's scared of them, too," Will said. "Everyone is. You can't…" He tried to grasp how to put it into words and came up short. The thing was, Guillaume and Ashton were beyond fear. You didn't even want to look at them wrong. At the beginning, apart from the 'accidents,' there had been reasons, as flimsy as they were, for killing people. There hadn't been a reason for Caleb. Not one that Will had heard, anyway.

"We gotta do it quick, too," Luca said. "Before *you*, Mr. Hunter, get all weak like the rest of us. You're strong enough to kill Guillaume."

"He has a knife."

"So take it away," Luca said.

"Ashton—" Will tried to find words for this, too. For how Ashton was, in some ways, scarier than Guillaume. He thought that maybe, without Ashton, Guillaume wouldn't have pushed that hard. It was like they were constantly trying to *impress* each other. Every time one of them did something fucked up, they'd look at the other one to see if their efforts were appreciated.

"Ashton's a stringbean, too," Luca said. "I bet you could take either of them. The rest of us will gang up on the one you don't get."

"I feel like this is a bad idea," Adam said.

"We can't do this shit diplomatically," Luca said. "That's how they got it from you, Adam. Because you kept trying to do shit diplomatically."

"The only thing that makes them scary is because they're willing to do stuff we aren't," Sage said, speaking, finally. He'd been quiet the whole time, staring into the fire. The twins still weren't back yet. Will thought the others would be worried, but maybe it was normal. Maybe it always took this long. Richard, too, was missing—but maybe he always was. Maybe he'd shown these guys where to camp and fucked off to wherever he spent his time. Richard was probably going to be the only one to survive this fucking thing.

"Then we gotta be willing to do that stuff," Luca said.

Adam swallowed, hard, and glanced around at them, and that was when they heard, from outside:

"Let us in, Luca!"

Luca muttered and hopped to his feet to go to what looked like a rope—closer inspection revealed it to be a mess of vines braided together—and hoisted. The twins ducked through and froze when they saw Will. "Hi," Reuben (probably) said. "You're here."

Will nodded a few times.

"He shows up," Luca said. "Pukes on the floor, cries a while, and then decides he's going to help us."

"Oh," Briggs (maybe) said. "Okay. Welcome, Will."

"Thanks," Will said. His voice still felt raw from the puke and tears, but if the twins noticed, they didn't say anything. Reuben dropped an armload of bananas, and Briggs had a small basket that looked weaved out of twigs and was full of eggs.

"I think some of these are even bird eggs," Briggs said, looking pleased with himself.

Luca nodded a few times and headed over to the fire. He made the eggs like he'd made them when Will had used to bring them to him, back when they all lived at the main camp—cracked the top open so they didn't burst, and then nestled them at the edge of the fire so that they could cook. "How do you guys get water?" Will asked.

"Ayers showed us a stream not too far from here," Luca said.

"We're thirsty, but we'll live," Sage said. Will nodded. He kept looking at Sage. Unlike Luca, who had grown hardened and prone to lashing out, or Adam, who seemed defeated, Sage was the same. Maybe it was because he'd seen violence before.

"You think you can eat?" Luca asked him. "Or are you going to puke all over the place again?"

"If there's not enough—" Will started, and Luca shook his head.

"No, Will," he said. "You're one of us now. We'll feed you."

×

And so began surveillance. As they watched, both James Howard and Jaxson Bates went down. James Howard was, according to Reuben and Briggs, who had witnessed it, a genuine accident. He'd slipped at the top of the waterfall and landed wrong. That didn't stop Kevin's guys from swarming all over him like piranhas and eating him, but he hadn't been killed on purpose. Jaxson Bates was another long one.

And then they caught Sage.

×

Will blamed himself. Of course he fucking blamed himself. If he hadn't come back, if he hadn't agreed with Luca that they needed to do something, Sage would have stayed safe. He wouldn't have been so close to the waterfall, and they wouldn't have caught him. More than that, they wouldn't have caught him when him and Will were out looking together. They'd split up. They'd planned to connect again when they were done watching.

And Vic Walsh had caught Sage.

If it had been Vic alone, maybe Sage could have talked his way free. Vic wasn't a bad guy—not normally. But Ryan Spencer and Nicky Wilder were with him, and the combination of Ryan's devotion to the cause and Nicky's cowardice must have done it. Ryan had Sage around the neck and dragged him toward the camp. Will's body jerked, like it wanted to chase them down, but he knew that he didn't stand a chance. Not against the three of them. Especially not with Ryan there.

So instead he followed.

The camp was mostly empty when they got back. No Guillaume or Ashton, so they tied Sage to a tree and waited. They chatted, a little. Will watched them. He tried to work up the courage to go over and untie Sage. Vic kept glancing over at Sage, and Sage himself was pale, and still, like he was trying to will himself out of this one, or at the very least, will himself to not think about what was happening, but the minute Will worked up the guts to go and free him, they came back.

They'd been out with Kevin, and they brought back a bunch of rabbits and birds, so Will guessed they were hunting. Ashton saw Sage first, exclaimed, and whacked Guillaume on the side of the head and pointed. Guillaume looked, and then he grinned.

"Vic found him," Will heard Ryan say.

Vic nodded. He was biting his fingernails.

"Awesome," Ashton said. Will was in a tree at this point, balancing himself as best as he could. He was closer to Sage than anyone else and so when Ashton and Guillaume got close, he heard and saw everything.

Ashton untied him and he collapsed on the ground. He tried to scramble to his feet, but Ashton grabbed his wrist and twisted it back until it was jerked up to the base of his neck. He had his other hand on the back of Sage's head, shoving it toward the ground. Sage was on his knees. "Gill, what do we do with this one?"

"We can have some fun," Guillaume said. Then he crouched beside Sage and said something in his ear, too quiet for Will to hear, but it made Ashton laugh and jerk Sage's wrist up farther until his arm broke. Sage did scream then. "Oh, c'mon, Horton. It's gonna get worse than that."

×

It did get worse than that.

×

Will didn't dare leave. He was sure that Luca thought that he'd turned Sage in himself or something; he didn't dare leave. He thought, and it was stupid, but he figured that the minute he left, Sage was dead. There was no saving Sage if he left. There was probably no saving him if he stayed, either, but at least—

Guillaume and Ashton were kicking him around like a soccer ball. Sage had his good arm protecting his head as best as he could. He only screamed when one of them stepped on his broken arm and when they were done, when they hoisted both of his arms above his head, tied them at the wrists, and threw the other end of the rope around a tree limb and secured it to the trunk.

If they didn't have anyone keeping watch…

The fire burned low and everyone was inside. Will dropped out of the tree and crept over to Sage, who was still awake, as far as Will could tell. Between the flickering light from the fire and the moon, Will could see bruises, and blood, and tear-streaks on Sage's face. "Sage," Will whispered.

"God, are you still fucking *here*?" Sage managed through gritted teeth. His voice broke. "Go. Get out of here. Go."

"I can—"

"You untie me and they'll figure it out," Sage said. "You—we won't make it back—they'll see us, follow us, and—"

"I can carry you, Sage," Will said. "You're not that big."

Sage was shaking his head. "Please, Will," he managed. "Please. Just go. Tell Luca and them that I got caught. Tell them that you guys have to be more careful."

"I can't—" Will started. "I can't—what'll Luca—"

He wanted to express it in a way that made sense, and that didn't sound stupid. He didn't just want to take Sage with because he was scared of what Luca would think; sure, he knew that Luca would scald him with his tongue if he irrupted back into the camp without Sage, but he also didn't want Sage to die. Sage was his best friend. Sage was the best person he knew.

Efrain going had been hard enough.

"Luca'll deal," Sage said. His jaw was tight. "They'll get bored and off me pretty soon, anyway. *Go.*"

"Sage—"

"Go, or I scream right now," Sage said.

"You—"

Sage shrieked and there was movement from the cave, and Will was off before he even realized what he was doing. He stopped running after some time and leaned against a tree, breathing hard. Sobbing. He was crying again. He felt like he'd cried more on this island than he ever had in his entire life, even when he was a baby. He eased himself onto the ground, to sit, and kept crying. He cried until he'd cried himself out, and then he wiped his face, picked himself up, and headed back to camp.

. chapter fourteen .

Luca took the news about Sage better than Will thought he would. Will came bursting in, as soon as the cover was lifted enough for him to squirm through, and told the story in a mess of consonants and vowels, and Luca and Adam and the twins listened, and then Luca snorted, stood up, and headed to the fire. He sat by the fire for a long time.

What he didn't do was accuse Will of orchestrating it. Will had been prepared for that, and when it didn't happen, it was like a weight lifted off of his chest. Adam put an arm around him. "Do you think we could get him out if all of us went?" he said.

"Maybe," Will said. "I—he didn't want me to try alone. If all of us are there he might…"

"He was still alive when you left, right?"

Will nodded. "Real beat up, but alive," he said. "Ashton broke—broke his arm."

Adam grimaced. "If we go talk to Kevin," Adam started, and Luca groaned, but Adam held up a hand. "Wait. Wait. *Listen.* For something like this, something this big—maybe he'll listen. Maybe he'll *have* to listen. All we want is Sage back, right? That's all we want. It's not like we're taking anything from them."

"Except a toy," Luca said. "That's what we're taking."

"I want to try," Adam said. "Please, let me try talking to Kevin before we go all guerrilla warfare on them."

Luca scowled, but he nodded. "But we're going now," he said. "Was Kevin there when you left?"

Will shook his head. He'd come back with Guillaume and Ashton, sure, but he'd disappeared back into the forest almost immediately and hadn't come back, even though it was late.

"Great," Luca said. "Maybe we can catch him hunting."

×

Will led the way to Kevin's usual hunting spots. The twins had stayed back at the camp—just in case they let Sage go and he staggered home, or something, they wanted someone there to let him in—and Luca and Adam followed Will. Will was trying to be quiet. He knew that Ashton and Guillaume were back at the camp, but...

"I see him," Luca hissed, and Will stopped short. Luca pointed. Kevin was crouched on the ground, tapping it with his stick. Adam cleared his throat, pushed his shoulders back, and called out:

"Kevin?"

Kevin jumped and whirled around, but he relaxed, a little, when he saw who it was. "What do you guys want?"

"So, Ashton and Guillaume have Sage," Adam said. "And he's not—Sage doesn't do anything to you guys. We haven't done anything to you guys. Can you get them to give him back?"

Kevin hesitated.

"Please," Adam said. "Please. You're not a bad guy, Kevin. If you were you wouldn't be out here so much."

"I wondered where you went," Kevin said, directly to Will, and Will shrugged.

"I couldn't do it anymore after Caleb," he said.

"Can I..." Kevin trailed off, and Luca must have glared at him, or something, because he looked at his feet and took a step back. "I can't do anything, you guys. I can't. If I say something—"

"If you say something, the other guys will follow you," Luca snapped. "Ryan Spencer. Vic Walsh. Nicky Wilder. We can't do anything against Guillaume and Ashton. You *can*."

"You guys are so fucking skinny," Kevin said. He shivered, a little, and shook his head. It was night-time, deep night-time; middle of the night, it felt like, but the moon was fat and full and heavy. "If I see you setting him free, no I didn't. But I can't..." He trailed off again. "Get out of here. Please."

As they walked away, Luca said to Adam, "So much for your fucking diplomacy."

×

Sage lasted a while. They weren't cutting him up, or anything. They were just beating the hell out of him and, as Ashton exclaimed one day, "Horton can take a hit!"

Always, Will or Luca or Adam was there, watching from a tree. Will was a little worried that Luca would end up going nuts and bursting in to rescue Sage and getting himself caught, too. Sage lasted a week getting pummeled and kicked and shoved around and spat on. He was jumped on and slammed against trees and more of his bones were broken. And someone was always watching him. That was the fucking thing. There was always someone, Nicky or Vic or Callum or someone, watching him to make sure nobody took him away. Guillaume was smart enough to know that they would want Sage back.

By the end, he was whispering pleas for them to just end it. He cried most of the time. Will, too, cried whenever it was his turn to watch. Will didn't know why they were still watching this all happen. Maybe because Sage deserved someone to watch and remember him.

Will would sure never forget him. Or the circumstances surrounding his death.

When he died, it was the same thing that Guillaume had done to Efrain, but he must've been practicing or something, because it was taking Sage a long time to die. His begging got louder and louder until Ryan Spencer bulled his way over, grabbed the knife, and cut his throat so deep his head almost fell off.

And then Sage was dead.

. chapter fifteen .

After Sage's death, after Will went back and told everyone what had happened, they barely left the camp. Richard Ayers brought them food and news. It seemed like every day he brought them a new name. Jonathan Ortega was caught crying himself to sleep and so Guillaume and Ashton cut off his head. Terrell Barron didn't come back from hunting—at least not in one piece. Callum Reid broke his arm and wasn't useful anymore and so they killed him. Lucas Johnson… well, he didn't do anything, as far as Richard could tell, but Guillaume and Ashton were getting bored. Tyler Murray, too. Same thing.

"So who've they got, then?" Luca asked, after nearing the news about Tyler. "Kevin, Ryan, Erik… Zach… Seth? Nicky?"

"Vic, still, and Leo, and Steven, and Johnny," Adam said listlessly. "Jeff. And Ashton and Guillaume."

"And us," Will said. "We're still alive. And Richard."

The thought that their numbers had shrunk to *nineteen* was insane. That was less kids than you saw in a classroom. More than half of them were dead now. They chewed on that, digested it, until Luca sighed and stood up. "Do any of you guys know if we're ever going to get rescued? Because I seriously doubt they're doing anything for that. What was your idea, Adam? Signal fire?"

"Any more smoke than we have right now would lead them right to us," Adam said. His voice broke. "We have a small fire on purpose."

"Fuck that," Luca said. "I don't care anymore. We've gotta get rescued. Ayers can't feed us forever. I'm building this shit up. Go find green branches."

When they hesitated, he shooed them off.

"*Go!*"

They scattered. Adam yanked the rope so they could leave, and it lowered behind them, and Will went scrambling for green branches. Luca was right, of course. If they didn't get rescued, they were just sitting ducks. And there was no way the main group was doing anything to try and get rescued. Probably Ashton and Guillaume didn't even *want* to get rescued. Probably they'd be happy if they slaughtered everyone else, until it was just the two of them, and then…

What? What would they do with just the two of them? Would they kill each other?

Will remembered the rumor that Ryan Spencer had told him, back before they'd crashed on the island, back when they were in school, when they were regular kids, that he'd walked in on them jerking each other off. Will couldn't really imagine Guillaume doing *anything* like that. Ashton, sure.

Guillaume? No way.

But there was something heightened, *intimate*, in the way they looked at each other when they were killing. When they were covered in blood. Will swore he'd seen Ashton lick blood off of Guillaume's fingers before.

He gathered an armful of green branches and made his way back and they built their signal fire.

×

Adam was right.

Smoke led them right to the camp.

×

They came at night, and when they couldn't figure out how to open the door that Luca had built, they pushed through. Ryan Spencer and Vic Walsh led the charge, and then they were there. Someone was screaming—the twins, or Luca, Will thought. He wondered wildly where Richard was before Kevin grabbed him and pulled him to his feet.

"*Run, Will,*" Kevin said through gritted teeth, and Will ran.

He didn't run far, though. He had to see.

He ran and then he turned and climbed the hill. He looked down. He watched as they forced Luca to his knees and cut him bad and he fell down, unresponsive. Adam was shrieking. The twins were sobbing.

Will didn't know if they figured that he himself had gone the way of Ayers of if he was just that unremarkable. If he didn't matter that much.

"Bring these ones to camp," Kevin said. The twins tried to fight but when you hit one of them the other one flinched, too, and anyway, they were outnumbered, and Adam fell silent, and before they all left, Ashton kicked dirt over the fire.

Before he followed them, Will ran back to the fire and relit it. He figured it was a long shot.

A long shot was better than no shot.

×

He also turned Luca onto his back and closed his eyes. Put his arms on his chest all crossed like you saw on dead people, and after thinking about it for a second, kissed him on the forehead. One more gone.

×

They played with the twins first. Made them hurt each other and everything. Tied them up. Most of the boys made a ring around them and Ashton and Guillaume were the center of attention. Will got as close as he dared, watching through his fingers, sometimes. He was crying almost constantly now. Everyone was too loud and nobody heard him. That's what he figured, anyway.

The twins died quick, and then they started in on Adam. They made fun of him and everything; taunted him. Ashton held him down and Guillaume cut off his hand. Adam passed out a little then, but Ashton hoisted him back up and his head was rolling and *then*—

"Holy fuck!" Ryan Spencer yelled, pointing toward the sky. "Is that a *helicopter*?"

Part Three: Guillaume Argot

After

. chapter one .

"*Gi-i-i-ill!*"

Ashton's scream ripped through the air like a bread knife through flesh and Guillaume stopped short. He'd gone upstairs, through a window, and there was a room at the end of the hallway and the light was on and Adam had to be there but if Adam was there then *who was downstairs with Ashton and—*

Ashton screamed again and it made Guillaume's choice for him. He turned and sprinted, running so fast his legs almost went out from under him and he nearly fell down the stairs and he skidded on his knees and then he was on his hands and knees next to Ashton who was bleeding and holding his guts in and Guillaume's fingers spasmed.

"Ashton?" he said. Ashton was shuddering, big, full-body shakes. He was breathing hard through his teeth. There was blood everywhere. Guillaume reached out and cupped Ashton's face. Ashton flinched, and then leaned into it, and then opened his eyes.

"Gill?" he said, and his voice broke. "Gill, I—I don't know—"

It was bad. It was really fucking bad.

"I'm dying, Gill," Ashton said. His voice was getting breathy and strange, and Guillaume looked back down at the blood and guts. There had been a time, Guillaume thought, when he would have enjoyed this. When he'd first gotten put in the hospital he'd replayed Ashton's testimony in his head over and over and over again.

We were all scared of him. He had a knife. He brought a knife.

We all helped, I guess, because if we didn't we'd be next.

I don't know. I don't know. He's crazy.

But Ashton had been so fucking good to him since. And even once he'd thought about it a little… one of them deserved to get away with it, right? Guillaume could take the fall because his dad could afford to get him into a nicer nuthouse. Ashton's parents had some money, but not like the Argots.

But Ashton was right. He was dying.

Guillaume pulled his knife out of his pocket and flicked it open. Ashton tracked it.

"I'm sorry, Ashton," Guillaume said. *I love you.*

Then he jabbed the knife right into Ashton's breastbone and leaned on it. Ashton screamed like a choir of angels. The bone split. Blood gurgled in Ashton's throat. Guillaume kept leaning. He cracked Ashton's chest open like a nut. Pulled out his heart. His hands were covered in blood, *Ashton's* blood, *Ashton*, and as he took a bite the light went out of Ashton's eyes.

It hit him then, as he swallowed, that he should have maybe asked Ashton who had unzipped his guts before splitting his chest cavity open and taking his heart. But that wasn't really the important part, was it? It wasn't important who had killed Ashton. What was important was that it had happened. What was important was that someone had taken him away from Guillaume.

His stomach rolled and he closed his eyes. Breathed through it. He had to eat the whole thing. He *had* to. It was the only way to keep Ashton with him.

He was pretty sure.

Dimly, somewhere, Guillaume knew something was wrong. Knew something had been wrong for a while. Knew that the nuthouse hadn't really made him better, *obviously*, but also that he hadn't *changed* like the rest of them had. Ryan had changed. Vic had changed. Richard had changed.

Ashton had changed.

Guillaume felt very much like he had when he was twelve. Like he had when he'd woken up drenched in sweat on the island. He wondered if the fever had cooked his brains too much and stunted him like this. He was bright academically but he'd *been* bright academically, back then. Nothing he did now wasn't something he could have done back then.

He took another bite and forced it down.

Ashton was growing cold.

A few more bites. Then he could go and get in the car and drive back to the hotel and take a shower and maybe have some Runts or something.

. chapter two .

Guillaume woke up and reached for Ashton instinctively before he remembered. The scream built in his chest but he didn't let it out; instead, he dug his fingernails so deep into his thighs he drew blood and pressed his face into the pillow and choked on nothing. Eating Ashton's heart had seemed so dreamlike he'd almost believed it was one for a minute.

    He tried to form the list in his head. Who it could be. Ryan was dead and Vic was dead and Richard was dead. Could be Nicky. They were in his neck of the woods. Could have been Adam, as unlikely as he thought it was; maybe the light on upstairs had just been a ruse.

    Who else was still around?

    Erik was, and Zach was, and Jeff was. He didn't think it was any of them. Same with Seth and Steven and Johnny and Leo.

    Will, maybe?

    Will would make sense. Guillaume still didn't know how Will had survived the island. He'd been there, in that camp, with Luca and Adam and them, and then he'd been gone. Slipped out somehow. Guillaume hadn't been thinking about Will at all. He really rarely did. Will was almost a nonentity. He was quiet, and Guillaume knew that he'd been pretty close with Sage, but…

    It was probably Will.

    Will or maybe Kevin. Guillaume had always had the feeling that Kevin had not been into everything he'd let Ashton and Guillaume to. But would Kevin kill Ashton like that?

Guillaume thought about it while he sat in the bath. He didn't like showers. He'd had to take showers in the nuthouse because some people went nuts and tried to drown themselves or whatever. Guillaume just liked to sit in water that was too hot and when he came out he was bright red like a lobster. When he'd been younger he'd used to read in the bath, a lot. He'd take in a stack of books and every time the water would get cold and the bubbles would fade he'd drain it and refill it. He'd spent Saturday after Saturday like that.

That was before him and Ashton. He'd tried to share that with Ashton, once, and he'd brought a stack of books and they'd sat in the jacuzzi but Ashton got bored.

A long, shuddering breath ran through Guillaume and he squeezed his eyes shut. Ashton had been his friend since the fifth grade. They'd gone to the same elementary school. It went through the eighth grade. There was a high school that it fed into. Ashton had moved to their school in the fifth grade. He hadn't gotten along well in public school and his parents, barely, made enough money to make it work.

Guillaume had been going to private school since pre-K and he hadn't made any friends. Ashton was different, though. The minute he came they'd stuck to each other. First he'd come right out and called Guillaume "Gill-ohm", which most of their classmates had learned very quickly was not Guillaume's name… but Guillaume didn't mind as much when it came from Ashton, especially when Ashton started calling him "Gill" and it made something weird bloom in his stomach. Teachers were mostly glad to have a person who would work with Guillaume… and who Guillaume would work with, too.

Maybe he would stop at a bookstore on his way home.

×

He got in Ashton's car and started off. He half-expected to be pulled over immediately. But maybe it was Ashton's turn to be blamed for everything. Maybe they'd find the body—because Guillaume hadn't taken it with—and decide it had been Ashton, except *EXCEPT* Guillaume had eaten his heart.

That was maybe something that they couldn't quite. Explain away.

If it was just Ashton.

But he wasn't pulled over, so he pulled into the parking lot of a Barnes and Noble and went and got a Frappuccino. He drank it and looked at his phone. Scanned news apps and social media. He found Will on social media.

Will was around. Will was in Michigan.

It had probably been Will.

He looked at Ashton's Instagram, too. Just because he missed him. He looked at all the pictures Ashton had posted when they were in Minnesota and Florida, and at college. He'd never really looked at these photos of himself like this before. Ashton captured him when he was reading, or doing homework, and he *always* made him look like he was something more than he was.

Then he shook his head, tossed his cup, and headed for the horror/thriller section to grab everything he hadn't already read. Horror was making a big resurgence, he knew that; there were so many books that had come out when he'd been locked up. He'd read his way through the entire library in the nuthouse and then his father had donated money to build a bigger library but they never bought anything *good.*

He came up with a good amount of books. He'd already read everything Stephen King had written because oftentimes they were the only horror novels the nuthouse stocked, but he could some Barker, and some Hendrix, and some Laymon. He bought *Exquisite Corpse* by Poppy Z Brite even though he'd already read it and already owned three copies of it because he loved it. Probably it was the best book ever written.

He paid with his dad's credit card and went back out to Ashton's SUV. He stacked the bags in the passenger seat and started home.

. chapter three .

He slipped in the back door at three in the morning. The house was so large that nobody would notice he was home. If he wanted, he could hole up in his room for a week and nobody would notice he was home. He didn't even know if his parents were around. They went off, sometimes. Europe, mostly. They had a house in Marseilles.

    He stole away, up to his bedroom. He'd spent a couple of months there after turning eighteen and getting out of the nuthouse. He hadn't been home since college had started, though. There hadn't really been a reason to be.

    Guillaume's bedroom was really very much the same as it had been when he was twelve. Red walls, black bedspread. Bookshelves and a desk. A desktop computer that still ran Windows 7. A flat-screen TV and horror movie Blu-Rays.

    He dumped his new books on the floor in front of his bookshelf and crawled into bed and slept for sixteen hours.

×

When Guillaume woke up his mother was in his room.

    "You're home," she said.

    Guillaume didn't say anything. He didn't know how she knew he was home.

    "Clarisse saw you on the cameras," she said. Guillaume stayed quiet. He didn't know they had cameras. "How long are you here?"

    Guillaume shrugged.

It was quiet, for a moment, and Guillaume wondered if she was going to say anything about the murders. If Ashton's body had been found yet. He would have to check the news about that. If Ashton had been found, that would explain why his mother was here.

But she didn't say anything else. She stood up and she left.

×

BODY OF "BOLIN TRAGEDY" SURVIVOR FOUND IN MICHIGAN HOME

Six years ago, sixteen boys aged 12-14 were rescued from Bolin Island, a small island in the Caribbean. Last weekend, the body of one of them was found eviscerated in the Michigan home of another.

Ashton Collins was nineteen years old and had just completed his first year of his college education at a small New England private university. He was an only child and he played a variety of sports in high school, though none of that transferred over to his one and only year of higher education.

Collins is not the first survivor of the Bolin Tragedy to have died this year. Ryan Spencer and Victor Walsh were both found dead in their homes, and while no body of Richard Ayers has been found, family and friends are worried something has happened to him as well.

"Richard's trusting," a source close to the boy said. "He would have gotten in a car with anyone. Whoever killed those other boys probably killed him, too."

It's unclear why Collins was in the home of Adam Nicholson, the boy who, six years ago, was hailed as one of the most heroic boys on the island. Nicholson was unable to be reached for comment.

One item of note is that Guillaume Argot, purported antagonist of the island, was released from a mental institution early last year. While he has been in no legal trouble, there are some that believe he might be trying to finish what he started.

×

"I didn't start it," Guillaume muttered, and closed his laptop. The sun was coming in through his window, which was closed, and the room had that baked, lived-in feeling that stuffy rooms in summer got. Neither of his parents had come up to talk to him since his mother had that first night. He was pretty sure they were gone. He fed himself by sneaking downstairs in the middle of the night for food. Mostly snacks, but he did, at one point, eat an entire log of smoked summer sausage.

    He was getting the itch, though. The article had one thing right: he might not have *started* it, but it was damn near time to *finish* it.

    He had a new list now, and Will would be at the very top of it. William Black. The background guy, the extra, someone of little to no consequence.

He would die beautifully.

. chapter four .

Guillaume went back to Michigan. He didn't take Ashton's car even though he wanted to. He had his own car. He left Ashton's car at his parents' house and figured that if they got sick of it they'd have it towed or something. Driving to do this was weird because driving had been Ashton's job and his job had been to slump in the passenger side seat and plan things and now he was a lone and even though the radio was jacked up *loud*—

It wasn't the same. He chewed consistently on Swedish Fish. He got one of those big family-sized bags from a Wal-Mart and kept it open on the passenger-side seat. Buckled it in so that it wouldn't topple over.

Back to Michigan.

Will Black lived in Munising. It looked like a small town and so it should be easy enough to find him. Maybe, if he was lucky, Adam would be there, too. Adam hadn't lived anywhere near Munising but maybe he was taking some comfort in Will.

Guillaume thought *that* was fucking ridiculous; Will had eaten just as many people as Guillaume had, almost, and he'd went along with everything, almost, even after they'd killed Efrain Foley, which Guillaume had thought would be his tipping point. Will had still gone along. Ashton hadn't liked Foley because Ashton had some kind of image of himself as someone entertaining, a class clown kind of guy, and Foley actually *was* a class clown kind of guy. Guillaume had thought that Ashton was funny but he knew that really nobody else had.

So killing Foley had been easy. He'd been on the bottom of the pecking order already, too, because he hadn't been a hunter, and so—

Will had stuck around after that. That had been the line for most of the other guys, for Adam and Luca and Reuben and Briggs, and of course Richard had already fucked off to god-knows-where, but Will had stuck around. He'd kept hunting. He'd kept eating.

So.

Guillaume drove up to Munising.

×

He stopped at a hair place and got his head buzzed.

×

It was on Lake Superior. Lake Superior was fucking huge.

×

There was a little bookstore and coffee shop and so Guillaume made that his first stop. He got a mocha with extra chocolate and then looked at the books. It was a fancy, almost literary sort of place, and so they didn't really have the kind of books he liked, but there was a nice copy of *The Iliad*, which was miles better than *The Odyssey* (Guillaume had read the former in the nuthouse and had dreams for weeks where Ashton was Achilles and he was Patroclus), and so he bought that and then took it down to the lake and read it. He wanted to get a feel for the town before he did anything. He wondered if it would be too suspicious if he started asking around for Will or if buzzing his hair was enough that nobody would recognize him.

He wasn't getting as many weird looks as usual. He was pretty sure it had worked. Guillaume'd been shaggy for practically forever.

He read most of *The Iliad* and then left it in his car and started walking. He sent a message to his guy that said WILL BLACK?

No response.

God, was he choosing *now* to get a fucking conscience?

Hissing, a little, Guillaume went back to Will's social media. He checked them all, and eventually, jackpot.

HIKING WITH MY MAIN MAN.

Both of them, hiking, at a place just a couple miles out.

It was time to finish this.

Or at least finish Will Black.

×

The road to the state park was bumpy, but Guillaume had an SUV, just like Ashton's, and so it handled well. Either way, Guillaume didn't much care if he wrecked it. He could buy another one. Also a large part of him was pretty sure he wasn't going to survive this.

Or if he did—

He wouldn't be coming back in this car. He might get Will, but Adam would get away and call the cops or something, and then even if he did get away—there were trees, it was forested, lots of places to hide, for sure—there was no way he could come back for his car. He'd have to wander through the trees until he got somewhere else.

The thought of dying didn't bother Guillaume. He didn't know if it ever really had, but after Ashton's death it had gotten worse. Last night he'd had to cut himself, right above his hipbones, to fall asleep. The only times he'd ever hurt himself when he was with Ashton had been when he'd wanted Ashton to do something.

Now he had blood sticking his T-shirt to his stomach. So, you know.

It was early enough that the parking lot had spaces, still, so Guillaume parked and got out of the car. He was wearing Doc Martens but he'd broken hem in so he figured they would work fine for hiking. It was a little warm for his hoodie but that was okay. He had his knife folded up nice in his pocket, and he shoved the pockets of his cargo pants with as much candy as he could handle, and then grabbed a twenty-four-ounce bottle of grape Faygo and went to the trail.

There were two loops that made one big loop. The full loop. It was eleven miles.

Probably he would have to do the full loop. Eleven miles sounded like a lot but hopefully he'd run into them long before he was even six or seven miles in. Besides, it was just walking.

You could walk forever.

. chapter five .

Several miles in and he was on cliffs and all he could see was water. He went up to the edge and looked down. It was a dizzying height. There were some people on the beach below but they looked like ants. Probably if he kept walking there would be a way to get down.

    The lake was so fucking *big*. It looked like an ocean. It reminded him of the island. Of looking out and seeing nothing but water for miles and miles and miles.

    He wished Ashton was here.

    The wanting, then, the *longing* hit him like a freight train and his heart stutter-stepped in his chest. Ashton was gone. Ashton was gone and never coming back. *Never*, no matter how many people Guillaume took care of, no matter how many times he hurt himself, Ashton was gone forever. Guillaume didn't believe in an afterlife, but in that moment he understood those who did. The longing was that deep.

    He closed his eyes for a minute. If he closed his eyes he could imagine that it was okay. That Ashton had scrambled ahead and was waiting for him. But even that wasn't good enough. He wondered if he would die if he threw himself off the cliff.

    Probably not at this part. The sand was probably too soft. He'd hurt, but if he wanted to be sure to die he should go and find a part of the cliff that overlooked the water directly. Then he could just let himself sink, and then it could be over, it would be over, and—

    "*Will!*" he heard, and it snapped him out of it.

    That had to be Adam Nicholson.

×

Guillaume melted back into the trees just a few moments before Will and Adam broke onto the cliff overlooking the beach. Will Black was well-built; sandy blond hair, broad shoulders, slim-hipped. He looked like he'd grown up to play high school and then college football. Adam, too, looked like he had recovered well from the island. Guillaume saw two hands, so one of them must have been a prosthetic.

He could shove them. Get at least one of them out of the way by sending them over the side of the cliff. But a part of him shied away from that. That was so fucking *impersonal*.

They were talking about him.

"I didn't see Argot," Will was saying. "But as soon as I stuck him Collins started screaming for him, so it's safe to say he was there somewhere."

"Like always," Adam said. He let out a long breath. "God, Sage shoulda let Guillaume die on that island."

Sage had helped him. Guillaume knew that much. Sage had tied up his leg and fed him water and found him antibiotics and he'd lived. Adam was right. Sage should have let him die. He hadn't repaid Sage back very nice. Sage had gotten the worst death on the island. Ashton had pushed for it. Guillaume thought he'd been jealous.

Guillaume had mostly wondered how much Sage could take. He was a tough kid.

Had been.

Their voices were growing fainter now. They were drawing away. Guillaume waited a few moments so that he wouldn't be seen or heard; there was really only one path that they could go on, and so he could be sure that he was following them. He would have to be quiet.

He could be quiet.

He would follow them deeper into the woods. On the cliff like this, especially above the beach, was no good. Once they went back into the trees—and he was sure the path went back into the trees—that's when he would go for it.

Once he couldn't hear them anymore, he stepped back onto the path and followed.

×

He couldn't see them anymore but he got used to that quickly. The path twisted and turned and he knew they had to be ahead of him. Besides, he kept scaling cliffs. That was the part he was on, was walking along the tops of cliffs and everything. The tug to throw himself off of them was gone now because he had a purpose.

A fucking *glorious* purpose.

Eventually, the trees came back. Guillaume was semi-certain that his scalp had burned. He kept reaching up for his hair and forgetting it was gone.

He'd only had his hair this short one other time. Right after the island. All of them had gotten shaved. After the helicopter had come, they'd taken Adam with, because of the fact that he was bleeding to death from his hand, his *stump*, and a couple of adults had stayed with them while a boat came for the rest of them. On the boat they'd all gotten their heads shaved.

Guillaume had been kept alone. On the boat. Ashton hadn't even come to see him. To see if he was all right.

He kept walking.

×

A prosthetic hand was hard plastic. So that had to be what had hit him.

. chapter six .

He was dazed, his eyes watering, but he was back on his feet. He could feel blood dripping down the back of his head to his neck and he was glaring. They were there. They'd laid some kind of—*trap*, he guessed.

Will stood with his arms crossed. Adam was the one who had hit him.

"You killed Ashton," Guillaume said. He directed this to Will.

"Yeah," Will said. "Creep deserved it."

"I—" Guillaume didn't know what to say, and he was moving faster than he was talking, because even before he cut himself off his knife was in his hands and he was lunging for Will. Will side-stepped him—his balance was wonky because of his head—and he whirled around a few times to avoid falling. He was breathing hard.

"Did you think we didn't figure it *out*?" Will said. "You guys go to Florida. Richard disappears. Dies, I'm assuming. You guys go to Minnesota. Vic dies."

"I didn't kill Vic," Guillaume said.

"So Ashton did. Whatever. It was fucking criminal what he got away with," Will said. "He was just as bad as you."

Guillaume tipped his head forward, partially because he agreed—Ashton'd had some image of himself as someone he wasn't. Guillaume knew who he really was and loved him for it, but Ashton liked to believe he was normal.

"You guys talked about me most," Guillaume said. "And I was ready to be the bad guy."

He reached back and touched the back of his head. His fingers came away bloody.

"Ouch," he said. "I'm bleeding."

Adam recoiled, a little, either because he'd made Guillaume bleed or because of his tone of voice. Guillaume didn't mind that he was bleeding. His balance and vision were still a little off, but that was all right. He could manage just as well. He had his knife and he had a willingness to do things they—

But Will had gutted Ashton like a fish.

So maybe Guillaume's willingness wasn't as big of a pro as he thought.

Adam was the weak point for sure.

So he lunged for Adam. Adam lashed out again with his prosthetic hand, using it as a battering ram or something, and Guillaume ducked under it. He stabbed out with the knife. It skipped across Adam's skin and got tangled up in his clothes. "God," Guillaume muttered. "Who wears this much to go *hiking*?"

Will grabbed him from behind and hoisted him away. His feet left the ground for a second and he kicked backward as hard as he could. He didn't care where he hit Will, but it ended up being somewhere soft and Will grunted and Guillaume hit the ground. He landed in a crouch and then turned and flashed out with the knife.

Will cried out.

"*Fuck*," he said, and Guillaume pulled the knife back and went for him again. He'd gotten him in the arm the first time, but he wanted a place where Will would die.

Will threw his arms up to protect himself and the blade stuck. Guillaume felt the jolt when the knife hit bone.

He didn't bother trying to pull the thing out. He just turned and ran.

. chapter seven .

Guillaume didn't know where he was going or where he even *was*, just that he was tripping over himself, over branches; he was no longer on the path, not by a long shot. He didn't have his knife anymore. Stuck in Will's arm, stuck *good*, and no more use to him. It wasn't the same knife he'd had on the island, of course, but he'd had a collection of the same knives at home, and he'd just taken one of those, and so—

So if he could get home, he could get another one and then—

He stopped short and looked around.

The problem was he didn't even know where the path was.

Panic started to claw at the base of his throat and he closed his eyes. Let his heart jump into his throat and *thought*.

If he could climb a tree and see the lake, he could walk toward the lake and then walk along the side until he came to the path. Because the path went along the lake. For a few miles.

But there were so many miles of Lake Superior coastline.

He could just turn around. He hadn't really turned, he didn't think. He'd just run. Probably Will and Adam were gone. They were probably going and getting medical attention for Will's arm.

He turned around and was greeted with a path that he'd made for himself.

Sighing, he rubbed the back of his head again and then pulled a bag of Nerds Gummy Clusters out of his pocket and ate as he walked.

×

Walking was boring. He daydreamed as he went.

×

When they'd been in fifth grade, the first year Ashton had gone to their school, they'd spent every weekend watching horror movies. Ashton knew more of them than Guillaume did and so Ashton would write lists and Guillaume would rent them all, one after another. Ashton would eat pizza and Guillaume would eat candy and—

The summer between fifth and sixth grade Ashton practically lived at Guillaume's house and they'd found a nest of baby birds and—

Sixth grade Ashton went out for football and it was the worst and—

×

"I fucking *got* you."

. chapter eight .

Adam shoved him up against a tree, his arm against Guillaume's neck. Guillaume didn't struggle. He didn't see Will. He didn't know where Will was. It probably didn't matter though. He stayed quiet.

He was exhausted.

Maybe it was the running, the miles of hiking, the fact that he'd done it all on Nerds and Swedish Fish and Faygo sodapop, or maybe it was because all of this had taken too long and wasn't even fun anymore. It had been fun when Ashton had been alive. Ashton had made it fun. Ashton had made it fun on the island, too.

But without Ashton, it was just revenge. And that wasn't fun.

"Kill me," Guillaume said. Adam's arm wasn't hard enough on his neck that he couldn't breathe or anything, and he could talk fine. "Kill me. Just fucking *end* it. I can't do this anymore."

Adam frowned at him.

"Is Will going to the hospital?" Guillaume said. "Are you going to tell them that I'm out here and I did everything? Tell them that Ashton was just a victim, too. I killed him the rest of the way, anyway."

"I thought you liked Ashton," Adam said.

"I loved Ashton," Guillaume said. The words tasted weird on his tongue. To say out loud to another person. "He was dying anyway. I ate his heart."

Adam swallowed rapidly.

"Either way, it's not his fault," Guillaume said. "It's mine. So fucking kill me."

Adam let him go and took a few steps back.
Guillaume figured they weren't too far from the cliff.

If Adam wouldn't do it, he'd do it himself.

Part Four: Adam Nicholson

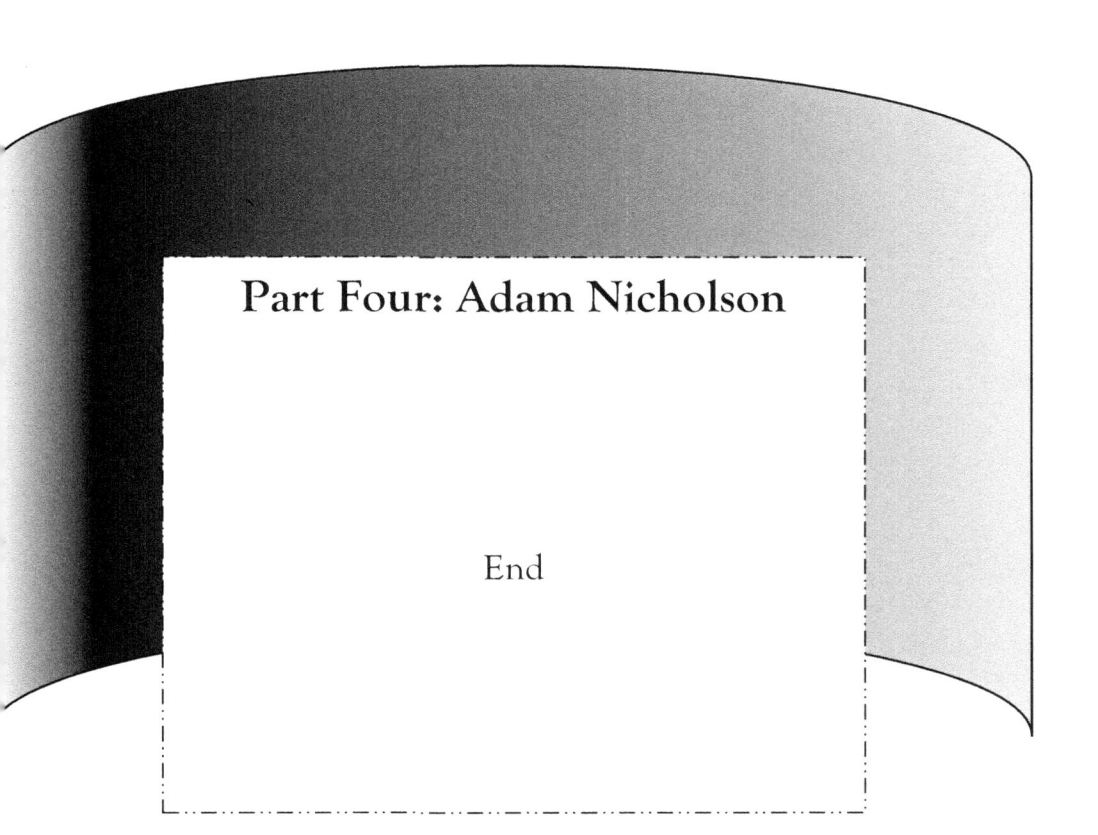

End

. fin .

Guillaume Argot had been his nightmare for the past six years, and he was an undersized, practically bald, nineteen-year-old with bad posture. In a fair fight, Adam had him for sure. And he *had* had him.

But then Guillaume started talking, and then Adam let him go, and then he was tearing through the trees, and all Adam could think was *Will's back there*, and so he followed.

Will sat on the edge of the cliff. Adam could see him, and he could see Guillaume running, scrambling, almost animalistic on all fours at points, and he knew what was going to happen the second before it did:

"*Will!*" Adam yelled. "He's *behind you!*"

Will jerked his head up and it was in that moment that Guillaume barreled into him and they both went over. Adam screamed, wordless, and then ran to the edge and looked off. Maybe there was some kind of ledge or something underneath.

There was. Will had landed on it—Adam could see him, looking bruised and bloody but mostly all right, leaning off of it, clutching at Guillaume, who was dangling. "Let me go," Guillaume snarled.

"No," Will said through gritted teeth.

"You *fucking gutted Ashton*, you can let me fall," Guillaume said, and Adam had to admit that he had a point with that one.

Will didn't let him go, though, and started dragging him back up. Guillaume had to weigh all of ninety pounds, tops, and Will and Adam weight-lifted between classes—they went to the same college—and so Adam was pretty sure that Will had it—

Will shouted, and Adam squinted, and—was Guillaume *biting* him?

He was.

Will let go and Guillaume fell.

×

Later, at the hospital.

×

Will had gotten stitched up and checked out. "It's gotta be over for good, now," Will said, frowning. "I mean, who's left that could even start killing people?"

"Kevin, I guess," Adam said.

But Will was shaking his head. "He wouldn't," Will said. "He… he didn't like what was going on any more than we did."

"But he did let it happen," Adam said. "And so—I mean, I know he didn't kill anyone, and you said that he was off hunting whenever they got started, but he *let* it happen. If he'd told Ryan Spencer to stop them, Ryan would've."

Will nodded a few times and looked down at his bandaged arm. "But we can keep moving on now," he said, and then he looked up and gave Adam a crooked smile. He held out his hand, and Adam took it. Squeezed it gently.

Guillaume was dead. Ashton was dead.

And they were still alive.

. playlist .

The Horror of Our Love – Ludo

The Greatest Story Ever Told – Ice Nine Kills

Destroy Me – Dr. Kitty

Casanova (C'est La Vie) – The Funeral Portrait

Bruises and Bitemarks – Good With Grenades

Madame La Mort – newhaven

The Phantom of the Opera – Mat Copley

Kiss Me You Animal – Burn the Ballroom

Jesus Don't Like That I'm Gay But Satans Cool With It – Lil Boodang

What Else Could He Be But a Jester – The Garden

Raging on a Sunday – Bohnes

Closer – Burn Season

This is Love – Air Traffic Controller

The Kid I Used to Know – Arrested Youth

Jalouse – Eskemo

Addict – Jacob Takanashi, Dave Capdevielle

Tentacles – Ghost Town

. author's note .

This book would not have been written without a few things, most notably, the novels *Lord of the Flies, Exquisite Corpse,* and *The Troop* (Most of Guillaume's opinions on literature mirror my own and FIGHT ME). Other than that, though, *Guillaume* is really a love letter to the Tumblr fandom of *Lord of the Flies* of roughly 2011-2014ish. I met some of my best friends through *Lord of the Flies* fanfiction (shoutout to Emma Riva, who provided the blurb for the back of the book, has been one of my greatest writing friends since she commented on a Rogice fanfic of mine back in like, 2011, and is the author of a great novel of her own titled *Night Shift in Tamaqua*), and I cut my writing teeth on those characters.

So *Guillaume* grew from that, I suppose. I've always loved stories inspired by *Lord of the Flies*. The best way to get me to be interested in a book is to compare it to *Lord of the Flies*. If it's compared, I will read it, and I'll probably like it. It was only a matter of time before I did my own "island book", but with a bigger focus on what would happen afterward. What would happen after a group of kids crashed on an island and then started killing each other and then got rescued? Like, what happens there?

There are a lot of in-jokes in this book. Ashton choosing "Roger Elwin" as a fake name for his roommate is probably the most obvious, but there are more if you look. This is, I think, the most deliberate book I have ever written, in a lot of ways, which is weird, because I didn't follow my usual writing process when writing this one. I've found that my best books are the ones that deviate a little.

Guillaume, I wrote about six thousand words, let it rest for a while, and then wrote the barest of outlines and lists of kids to kill. When Ashton referenced kids and how they died, I picked randomly—I didn't know what was going to happen during the island section until I wrote it.

And then, naturally, really liked the characters I'd written to kill (Luca, Efrain, Sage, most particularly), but that's how it always works, right?

At this point, I think this is the best book I've ever written. I also think it's the only book of mine that I can confidently call a horror novel. Is it… *extreme horror?* I don't know, but preteens do like, eat each other, so maybe. I loved writing this book. I only hope you loved reading it as much as I loved writing it.

Printed in Great Britain
by Amazon